Sugar RUSH

COULSON'S WIFE

COULSON'S CRUCIBLE

COULSON'S LESSONS

COULSON'S SECRET

COULSON'S RECKONING

UNLOCKED HEARTS

SUNDERED HEARTS

AFTER SUNDOWN

WHILE SNOWBOUND

SUGAR RUSH

UNLOCKED ❦ HEARTS

Sugar RUSH

Anna J. McIntyre

Sugar Rush
(Unlocked Hearts Series)
A Novel
By Anna J. McIntyre
Cover Design: Elizabeth Mackey
Editor: Suzie O'Connell

ISBN: 978-1-949977-47-9

To my dad, Walt.
Your special hot fudge recipe has always been a favorite with family and friends. I hope you don't mind me stealing the recipe for this book! I know you never cooked yours in the microwave, but I really did figure out a way to make Walt's Hot Fudge on Demand Mix. I loaned that recipe to my character, Lexi. And I loaned your name to Lexi's dad.
Love you.

"**I** want you to marry Jerome Peters."

Her grandfather's decree was not what she expected to hear. When summoned to his study to discuss her future, Lexi had naturally assumed the topic would focus on career plans, now that she was finished with college.

"Are you serious?" The phrasing of her question was all wrong. Lexi realized that immediately. No one would describe Ethan Beaumont as a jokester.

The elderly man sat rigid in the leather wingback chair. He did not respond to her outburst. As was his habit, he rested his elbows on the chair's arms, the fingers of his hands laced together, absently tapping the knuckles against his narrow chin. Silently, he studied his granddaughter's expression.

Another man might look overdressed in the three-piece gray silk business suit, considering the home setting—but not her grandfather. The fact he wasn't wearing the jacket didn't make him look any less dignified and formal. The years had been kind to Beaumont, who—at age 81—still had a full head of gray hair. If he had lost height due to the passing of time, it proved insignificant, for he still stood over six feet. There was a slight slouch to his posture, yet his overall physical appearance was sturdy and solid.

"I discussed it with him when we were in Europe, and he agreed you'd make a suitable partner, especially now that you've finished college. Your marriage would secure the future of the company."

"Grandfather, I barely know Jerome Peters. Not to mention the fact he's old enough to be my father."

"Don't be ridiculous, Lexi. You've known Jerome all your life. Plus, a girl your age needs an older man to guide her."

"Umm, Grandfather, you do know we live in the 21st century?"

"Don't be impudent, girl," he snapped.

"I'm sorry, Grandfather, but I'm not marrying Jerome Peters. I wouldn't even go out on a date with the man, much less marry him."

"Don't be hasty, Lexi. That's a trait you inherited from your father. Hasty decisions never served him well."

"You mean because he married my mother?" *Maintain composure,* Lexi silently reminded herself.

"Precisely. I'm pleased to see you understand."

"My father loved my mother."

"Perhaps, but no good came of it."

I suppose that includes me. I must be a constant disappointment to you, Grandfather.

"Lexi, I didn't call you here to discuss your parents' misfortunes. We're here to discuss your future, and I don't want you to make the same mistakes as your father. It's obvious you're too young and immature to make the right choices. We all have duties, Lexi. You have one to this family."

"I'm sorry, Grandfather." That wasn't entirely true. Lexi was not a bit sorry. "I really don't understand how marrying a man I barely know—and don't particularly like—has anything to do with duty toward family. Perhaps it will in some way help your business, but I'm afraid I'm not willing to throw away my life for your company."

"You have two choices. You behave as a Beaumont should and marry Jerome and work very hard to be a good wife, or you leave this house, and don't ask me for anything, ever again."

"You're kicking me out?"

As threats go, Lexi didn't find this one especially intimidating. Her grandfather always expected things to be on his terms, and everything came with a price. Since she wanted a degree in graphic design, she had followed his rules without complaint. During the school term, she had lived in the dorms and spent the summer and holidays at her grandfather's estate, typically alone with the servants.

Her final term had ended days before Christmas. There hadn't been a ceremony to commemorate her graduation—*with honors*—earning a Bachelor of Science in Graphic Design. Even if there had been, it was doubtful her grandfather would have attended. As it was, he wasn't even home for Christmas. He was in Europe on business and had just returned home this morning.

Lexi had had no idea he was coming home that day and had been on her way to help her best friend, Angie, with a photo shoot, when her grandfather's housekeeper stopped her at the front door.

"Your grandfather got home early this morning," the housekeeper had told her. *"He wants to see you imme-diately."*

Lexi had given Angie a quick call on the cell-phone, before going to her grandfather's study. It was just an informal photo shoot, and they were planning to have some breakfast first, so neither girl was particularly upset about the delay. Lexi hadn't intended to tell her grandfather about her plans until she landed a job—one with a regular paycheck. Then she would sit down with the elderly man and let him know she would no longer be living under his roof—or under his control. Of course, she hadn't intended to point out the latter part.

Lexi expected her grandfather to object to the

move. But now, here she was, sitting across from him in the study, and he was threatening to kick her out, something she was more than willing to do on her own.

"Okay Grandfather," Lexi said calmly, standing up and clutching her large handbag. "If that's what you want, I'll move out."

An unpleasant smile played on Ethan Beaumont's thin lips. Narrowing his eyes, he studied his granddaughter. "I don't believe you fully understand the consequences," he said in a low menacing tone.

"You want me to move out or marry your business partner. Yes, I understand. I'll go pack my things now, and I'll move out today."

"No, Lexi. You will not pack *your* things. I paid for your things. I paid for your car; it's in my name. If you make this choice, you'll walk out that front door now, and don't come back. Be grateful I gave you an education. That is certainly more than what you arrived with."

"Are you saying I can't get my clothes? My personal belongings?" Knowing her grandfather, she wasn't especially surprised about the car. She had already discussed it with Angie.

"If I move out, Angie, Grandfather won't let me keep the car. I need to be prepared to take public transportation or walk to work, until I can afford to buy one. Maybe I'll get a scooter," she had told her friend.

"But the car was a high school graduation gift!" Angie had countered.

"I know my grandfather. If he decides he doesn't want me to move out, he'll dangle the car in front of me as a possible punishment. I'd be surprised if he didn't."

What had surprised Lexi was the business with Jerome Peters and the fact her grandfather intended to hold her clothes and other personal belongings hostage. With surprising calm, Lexi walked from the study, leaving her grandfather sitting on his leather perch like a predatory hawk. Refusing to look back, she walked to the front door and out of her grandfather's house.

Terrified he might snatch her handbag from her grasp; she picked up her pace and walked as fast as she could without actually running from her grandfather's estate. Of all her worldly possessions, the ones in her oversized purse mattered the most to her.

There was her digital camera, which was more than just a camera—it was a source of income. Unbeknownst to her grandfather, she had been submitting photographs and vector images to stock photos sites for the last three years. Each month her income grew, and she was now earning over $500 a month. It was hardly enough to live on, but it was an income stream.

Also stuffed in the oversized purse was her laptop computer. While in art school she had purchased a number of graphic software programs at the student rate—a necessary educational expense. Had her grandfather thought to confiscate the computer, it would cost her thousands of dollars to replace the programs alone. She was certain he assumed her computer and camera were upstairs in her room with the rest of her personal belongings.

He had no idea she had opened her own bank account when she turned eighteen and had been stashing money away each month. As far as he knew, the only cellphone she owned was the one on his cell plan. She was confident he would have her phone disconnected by the time she reached the end of his driveway. It didn't matter. She had purchased her own cellphone, with a separate number, several years earlier. Ethan Beaumont had taught his grand-daughter one invaluable lesson in the last eleven years—whatever Ethan Beaumont gives, he does so with conditions.

She just had no idea, until now, how extreme those conditions could be. When she reached the sidewalk, she pulled the cellphone from her purse and called Angie.

"Can you pick me up?" Lexi asked when Angie answered the phone.

"Is there something wrong with your car?"

"I don't have a car, remember? It belongs to my grandfather."

"You told him!"

"Not exactly. But he's kicked me out of his house."

"I don't understand."

"I'll explain it all when you pick me up. I'm walking in the direction of your apartment, so if you could just come get me, I'd really appreciate it."

"Would you like breakfast now, sir?" the housekeeper asked Ethan Beaumont as he strode out of his study, making his way to the staircase.

"No. But call J.B. Tell him to get over here immediately," he snapped.

Ethan climbed the staircase and went straight to Lexi's room. He found her bed carelessly made, as if she had rushed out that morning in a hurry. Glancing around the room, he took visual inventory of her belongings. It seemed to be mostly clothes, shoes, and a few books. Jerking open drawers in her dresser, he rummaged through each one before going to the next. Opening the closet doors, he found her clothes neatly on hangers and several boxes tucked on the top shelf.

In the adjoining bathroom, he found her robe hanging on the back of the bathroom door, and a toothbrush, toothpaste, shampoo, and conditioner sitting on the counter. The only sign of makeup was a mascara smudge on the sink. Going back into the bedroom, he walked to the window and looked outside. He saw her car parked in the driveway; she had obviously not tried to challenge him on that point.

There was a soft knock on the door.

"Yes?" he called out. The housekeeper opened the door slightly and timidly peeked in.

"Mr. Barnett said he'll be right over."

"Helen, do you know where my granddaughter keeps her computer, her camera?"

"If it isn't in her room, I imagine she has it with her." Helen opened the door wider and stood in the doorway.

"Damn. Helen, I want you to box up all my granddaughter's belongings. Store them in the carriage house for the next week. If she doesn't return, put them out with the trash. And you're not to give her any of the boxes unless you check with me first. Do you understand?"

"Yes, sir." Helen didn't understand.

CHAPTER TWO

Jeff Barnett sat patiently in his car, waiting for the light to change. His fingers absently tapped on the edge of his steering wheel, in rhythm to the song playing on the car's radio. The windows were down, letting in the cool breeze. It was a sunny January morning, and the few white clouds in the sky were quickly dissolving into the blue canvas. If the weather reports were accurate, by mid-noon the temperatures would reach the seventies.

He watched as a young woman hastily traversed the crosswalk, impatient to reach her destination. Draped from her right shoulder was an oversized leather handbag, which she clutched possessively. He noticed she kept looking behind her, as if she worried about someone following her. He found himself glancing in the direction she kept looking, but saw nothing suspicious.

The oversized bag looked awkward on her small frame; he doubted she was even five-feet, five-inches tall. Forgetting for a moment the local high school was out for winter break, he first assumed she was a high school student late for class, and the bag held her books.

When she reached the middle of the crosswalk and glanced his way, he realized he had guessed wrong. He knew that face. While he had never seen her in person, he had spent enough time admiring her portrait in his employer's office. She was Ethan Beaumont's granddaughter, Lexi Beaumont.

Jeff wondered where she was going in such a hurry and why she was walking. He and Ethan had just arrived home from Europe early that morning, and he was under the impression Beaumont was anxious to see his granddaughter, so he was surprised that his employer had summoned him to the estate. Jeff would have appreciated some down time, but as Ethan Beaumont's executive assistant, that was rarely possible.

Jeff wasn't too annoyed at the summons, because he assumed this would be his opportunity to meet at last, Lexi Beaumont. He had been working for his current employer for almost two years, and in all that time, he had never met the young heiress. Either she was off at school or—when she was home for the holidays or summer break—he was typically at one of the company's European offices, handling some situation for his employer.

While observing Lexi, he heard a horn honk, and both he and Lexi glanced toward the sound. A red Volkswagen bug had pulled up along the curb in the cross street. He looked back to Lexi and noticed she was now smiling and waving at whomever was in the car. It was obviously her ride. That somewhat explained why she didn't have her car, but he wondered briefly why her friend hadn't picked Lexi up at the estate.

Perhaps she simply enjoyed a morning walk. He did. Of course, that didn't exactly fit the picture he had of Lexi Beaumont, as described by her grandfather. Some girls enjoyed a vigorous hike in the fresh air, while others enjoyed a comfortable ride in a limousine. According to Ethan Beaumont, his granddaughter was the second type of girl.

She was dressed casually in denims, hoody and jogging shoes. He wasn't sure what she wore under the hoody. He would never have expected her to be out in public dressed like this. The Lexi Beaumont he had heard about was a high maintenance ball of fluff —sexy and cute, but more an accessory on some man's arm that an intelligent, independent woman. From what Jeff knew, this girl would be more comfortable wearing trendy designer clothes and stylish but uncomfortable high heels and certainly not carrying that enormous handbag.

When discussing his granddaughter, Beaumont insisted he loved her and only wanted what was in her best interests, yet explained he knew her limitations and purpose. While Jeff was never attracted to empty-headed nymphs, he liked to look, and even in the casual garb, Lexi Beaumont was nice to look at.

The light turned green seconds before Lexi reached the Volkswagen. Jeff was just driving through the intersection when she got into the car. A few moments later, he glanced up into his rearview mirror and watched the Volkswagen drive off in the opposite direction.

THE MASSIVE WROUGHT IRON GATE GUARDING THE front entrance to the Beaumont estate was open when Jeff arrived a few minutes later. He turned into the private lane, driving his car over the red-paver driveway leading up to the main house.

He immediately noticed the silver Honda Accord parked along the edge of the drive. That was probably Lexi's car, he guessed. Perhaps Ethan was punishing his granddaughter for not parking the automobile in the garage, which would explain her morning walk. Ethan Beaumont was almost obsessive about parking his cars in the rear garage.

Jeff found his employer waiting for him in the

study. The elderly man sat behind his oversized mahogany desk, talking on the phone, when Jeff entered. Ethan waved him into the room and pointed to the chair facing the desk.

"I believe I saw your granddaughter," Jeff said, when Ethan finished his call and placed the handset back in its cradle.

"Did you? How did you know it was her?" Beaumont studied his young assistant.

Barnett hadn't changed his clothes since the two parted ways early that morning at the airport. The younger man still wore tan slacks and a red-and-tan golf shirt. He hadn't had an opportunity to shave in over 24 hours, and the thick stubble covering his normally clean-shaven face distracted from his preppy look. Even his neatly trimmed, light brown hair looked uncharacteristically disheveled.

Not as tall as Beaumont, the twenty-six year old assistant's stocky physique barely reached 5' 11" in height. Regular trips to the gym kept the younger man's muscular body in prime shape.

"The portrait," Jeff explained.

"Yes, that portrait is a remarkable likeness. Excellent artist. Where did you see her?"

"She was getting into a red Volkswagen, at the Mission and Third Street intersection."

"Ah, very good. Then you're ahead of the game."

"Excuse me?"

"That's why I called you here. You're the only one I trust to handle the situation."

Jeff didn't respond. He sat, silently listening, curious about how getting a glimpse of the granddaughter had anything to do with his job.

"What I'm about to tell you is to be kept in the strictest confidence."

"Certainly, sir." Jeff sat up a little straighter in the chair, focusing on every word.

"It's been arranged for some time that my granddaughter and Jerome Peters are to be married."

Jeff didn't respond to the news, although it wasn't what he expected to hear. Jerome Peters was much older than Lexi and not a particularly handsome man. Actually, that was a bit of an understatement. Behind Peters' back, Jeff overheard a couple of the women from the office refer to Peters as a troll. Beaumont's partner was, however, a very wealthy man. Attractive young women often agreed to marry rich older men, even when those men looked like trolls.

"Let's just say the girl has had a change of heart. Lexi's always had a bit of a rebellious streak, like her father. Of course, I can't let that personality flaw destroy her future, as it did my son's. Soon, she'll discover she was behaving rashly and come back home and do what is the best for her future. In the meantime, I can't have the vulnerable girl exploited by some opportunist who might seduce her or lead her down some unsavory path. I need you to keep an eye on her, and report back to me what she's doing."

"You want me to spy on her?" Jeff asked, trying to conceal his distaste for such an assignment.

"I want you to put her under surveillance. You have the necessary technical skills. I'm sure you're perfectly capable of setting up some sort of concealed recording device. I don't want her to know she's being watched. It's for her own good."

"Yes, sir." Jeff shifted uneasily in the chair, wondering how long this little assignment would last. While he wouldn't mind spending time watching the lovely, yet not-too-bright Lexi Beaumont, the thought of bugging the girl made him uncomfortable.

"The red Volkswagen belongs to her friend, Angie. That will put you ahead of the game; we now know where she went. Before you leave, I'll get you the address. I imagine she called Angie from her cellphone, when she left here, asking for a ride. I suppose I should have anticipated that and had her cellphone disconnected. I'll take care of that later."

"I don't understand."

"My granddaughter's had it very easy since she moved here. She thinks that, now that she has graduated from college, she's free to do whatever she wants. That is technically true, of course, but she doesn't realize that to earn her freedom, she can't expect me to pay her way. When she learns the world is not so easy when someone isn't picking up the tab, she'll be back and do what is ultimately best for her future. Someone like her can't survive on her own. Unfortunately, she's just like her mother. I need to teach her a lesson, before she gets herself in serious trouble. That's why I need you to keep an eye on her. Report back to me; let me know what she's planning."

Beaumont's words sounded a little odd to Jeff. *Didn't he just say she was like her father? Is she like her father, mother, or both?* Jeff wished he had the luxury to tell Beaumont that babysitting or playing private eye wasn't part of his job description.

Unfortunately, he couldn't risk abrupt termination. In the current economy, finding a decent job proved more difficult when unemployed. He understood how lucky he had been to land such a well-paying position after completing his Master's Degree. Perhaps it wasn't his dream job—it involved tedious tasks, however it did include interesting travel and good medical benefits.

Beaumont handed Jeff a debit card and told him how much he could spend. Jeff thought the budget was excessive, considering the task. Ethan rummaged through some index cards on his desk, until he found what he was looking for. He handed a card to Jeff. It was the contact information for Lexi's friend, Angie.

"Assuming Lexi will be staying with her friend, I

want you to rent an apartment at Angie's complex. Try to get one as close to her unit as possible. Lexi will undoubtedly be staying there. Purchase whatever you need to set up surveillance.

"As soon as you can verify she's there and has her computer and camera with her, contact me immediately. I'll be filing theft charges this afternoon and will need to know where she and the stolen merchandise are."

"You're having your granddaughter arrested?" Appalled, Jeff forgot to conceal his reaction. Ethan only chuckled at the response.

"Don't worry. I don't intend to have her actually hauled down to the police station and locked up. I don't believe Jerome would care for a wife with an arrest record, and I certainly don't want our family name tainted. It's just to scare her a little and force her to give up her precious electronics. If she wants a fancy computer and camera, she can get a job and buy her own. Consider this necessary character building."

"Once you file charges, won't they have to take her in?"

"Perhaps I misspoke. Technically, I'm not filing charges at this time. Just a nice chat with the police chief, who is an old friend of mine."

Jeff was relieved Ethan Beaumont didn't intend to have the granddaughter arrested. Had that been the case, he would be forced to turn down the assignment and risk losing his job. It would be difficult to find a new position if his former employer refused to give him a recommendation, something that would probably happen if he crossed Beaumont.

As he left the estate, the housekeeper approached him and passed on some disturbing information regarding Lexi and her grandfather. It heightened his hesitancy about the unsavory assignment.

Reluctantly, Jeff followed his boss's instructions. His first stop was to the bank to pull out some cash using the debit card Beaumont had given him. The next stop was an electronic shop to pick up surveillance equipment. Questions of moral ethics and the legality of using such equipment made him uncomfortable, yet he made the purchase. The final stop would be the Hillcrest Apartments, where Angie lived, to ask about vacancies.

CHAPTER THREE

"I still find it hard to believe, even for your grandfather," Angie said as she led the way into her apartment and tossed the keys on her kitchen counter. Lexi followed her friend and closed the door behind them. "Isn't Jerome Peters that creepy little man who finds it impossible to keep his hands to himself?"

"I'm afraid so. But to his credit, he's never *accidentally* touched me when Grandfather was in the room."

"Gross. And your grandfather expected you to marry him?"

"I confess; this one totally caught me off guard. While walking to meet you, I kept running the morning over in my mind, asking myself how I might have handled the situation differently. But I couldn't come up with anything."

"I still can't believe he kept your clothes! What does he think he's going to do with them?"

"I imagine he'll throw them away. I really don't care about the clothes, but I have a couple of boxes in my closet upstairs that I should have grabbed. But I was so desperate to get out of there before he asked for my computer and camera—since he paid for those, like he did the car."

"I thought they were birthday gifts."

"Yes, all three were gifts, but Grandfather giveth, and Grandfather taketh away."

"The old bastard. What was in the boxes?"

Although Lexi considered Angie her best friend, they had known each other for less than two years, having met during their junior year at college. They had initially met at a party hosted by a mutual friend. Once they realized they were both going to the same school and each would be graduating in December instead of June, they had decided to see what else they had in common.

Lexi had majored in graphic design and Angie in photography. Angie came from a close-knit family, with supportive parents and overbearing brothers, while Lexi had been raised by her wealthy and emotionally detached grandfather.

"Some sentimental stuff from my parents. After they were killed, Grandfather hired someone to clean out our house—got rid of everything—before selling the property. He never even asked me if I wanted anything, and I was still in shock. I never thought to ask. Hell, I was only ten at the time."

"So, what was in the boxes, if he got rid of everything?"

"My parents had some really close friends, Joe and Carolyn Manning. They didn't have kids, but I remember they were always nice to me, and they often vacationed with us. I remember one year going to Hawaii. It was a blast.

"After my parents' funeral, I only saw them one other time. They stopped by my grandfather's house. It was probably a month after the funeral. Grandfather was on one of his business trips, and I was left with the housekeeper. They brought me two boxes, filled with random stuff like photographs and some things Mom had loaned Carolyn, but had never been returned.

"Carolyn and Joe stood up for my parents when they eloped, and she had some great pictures. Those were in the boxes, along with photos from trips we'd all taken. Fortunately, I scanned all the pictures a long time ago, so those aren't really lost to me, but I would like to get the originals back."

"Lexi, if you say your grandfather sold your parents' house, wouldn't that be your money?"

Lexi laughed ruefully at the question. "I asked him that when I was in high school. I confronted my grandfather once, and he informed me my father had borrowed a considerable amount of money from him.

When my parents died and their estate was liqui-dated, all proceeds went to pay off my grandfather."

"I really don't understand how you've been as nice to him as you have all these years, considering the mind games he loves to play."

"It's all about control. Grandfather has an obses-sive need to control everything around him. He tried it with my father and failed. I'm all he has left."

"I never understood why your parents appointed him as your guardian, especially considering their relationship with him. Hell, my sister-in-law made a point to make me guardian of her and my brother's son, if something happened to them. She said her parents would be the last people she'd want to raise Joey."

"I suppose my dad loved his father. Maybe he felt Grandfather was in the best position to give me what I needed financially, since my parents died broke. And I suppose that was true, to an extent. I went to good schools; I never went hungry. And even though he took the car back, he can't take away my educa-tion. I'm pretty lucky to have a degree and no student loans."

"True. And you still have your computer and camera, which will help generate some income until you land a job. You can stay with me, like we planned."

"Something about the computer and camera is bugging me."

"What do you mean?"

"I don't think my grandfather expected me to walk away from the car so quickly. I've a feeling he assumes I'll come home after I think about it. But I won't, and knowing him, he'll start obsessing on the camera and computer. I have this gut feeling he'll want them back."

"Well, tell the old bastard to shove it, because they belong to you now!"

"I suppose, but just in case," Lexi opened her bag and removed the laptop. She placed it on Angie's kitchen table and turned it on. The password to Angie's Wi-Fi was already in the computer, so when the laptop powered on, it immediately connected.

"What are you doing?"

"I'm going to move some of my files to my Dropbox and change some security settings. If my Grandfather finds a way to get this back—and knowing him, he will—I don't want any of my personal files left behind."

"Now you're just being paranoid," Angie scoffed. "If he was going to take it away from you, he would have already. Anyway, I'm not about to let that old bastard into this apartment."

"I've just learned to never underestimate my grandfather. Plus, I find it especially unsettling that I didn't see the Jerome Peters thing coming. He totally slipped that one by me. This is precisely the reason I got my own cellphone."

"I always thought it was kind of strange, having two phones, especially when your Grandfather was paying the phone bill."

"Right, and the minute he's mad at me, he yanks away the phone, and all the numbers I've saved are gone. I don't think so. Did you forget the story I told you about how quickly he sold Cricket when I got in trouble at camp?"

Angie remembered hearing about the incident. It had been devastating for Lexi, to lose the horse she loved, especially so because her parents had given it to her the year before their death. But her grandfather had stubbornly sold the animal, insisting he had every right, since it was his money that paid for the horse's keep, and if she could so easily throw away money he spent on camp, then she didn't deserve the horse.

It was true that she had never wanted to go to camp—that was something Ethan insisted she do each summer. He certainly didn't want a young girl underfoot when school was out. But she hadn't caused the incident that had gotten her sent home. She was the victim. Ethan Beaumont wasn't interested in some story about how the orphan had become the target of several rich girls, teased unmercifully and forced to endure one cruel prank after another, until one prank caused a fire in the dorm, and they blamed Lexi. Without a guardian's support, no one was interested to hear her side of the tale. The next summer, she went to a different camp.

"When looking back, I think the worst part was that Grandfather made me feel guilty, as if my actions forced him to sell her. Now that I'm older, I understand he was looking for an excuse to get rid of her. He planned it all along. He was just waiting for me to slip up so he could use it as one of his *lessons*. Had it not been the trouble at camp, it would have been something else."

When Lexi finished removing the files from her laptop and updating her security settings, she turned the computer off.

"You don't have to work at all today?" Lexi asked.

"No. I cancelled the photo shoot after you called the second time."

"Then, do you think you could take me to the mall? I need to pick up some clothes, a toothbrush, and a few other things."

"It's too bad we don't wear the same size, then you could just borrow some of my clothes for now and slowly build your wardrobe."

"The only thing I'm getting at the mall, in the way of clothes, is something nice to wear on a job interview and some underwear. I thought we could stop at the thrift store after the mall. For now, this girl is dressing budget. I'm not about to blow my savings on a new wardrobe."

JEFF WAS RATHER PLEASED WITH HIMSELF. THE apartment complex had a number of vacancies, including a furnished unit across the walkway from Angie's apartment. The Hillcrest Apartments was one of the few complexes in town that rented short-term. Confident the manager would run a background check and see he was already renting an apartment nearby, Jeff told the manager he only needed the unit for the rest of January, as his place was under renovation. The moment he told the falsehood, he regretted it, realizing he had no idea if the manager had any knowledge of his complex. When the manager didn't seem that interested in the information, Jeff told himself he was being paranoid. *I'd make a crappy spy.*

He wasn't sure what he was going to do or how he would proceed. Although he was tech savvy and would be perfectly capable of bugging the apartment or hacking into Lexi's computer, he wasn't prepared to do either of those things, in spite of the fact he had already purchased the items necessary to bug the apartment.

Since leaving the Beaumont estate that morning, he had cooled considerably at the notion of playing spy, yet understood he couldn't walk away without the risk of losing his job. For now, he would keep an eye on Lexi—from a safe distance—and hopefully, she wouldn't get herself in too much trouble, thus jeopardizing his job.

Lexi and her friend Angie were just leaving the apartment when he was unlocking the door to the unit he had just rented. He quickly ducked into his apartment and shut the door behind him, leaving it open just a crack so he might overhear the girls as they walked by the door.

From their conversation, it was obvious they were on their way to the mall. A moment later, he looked outside and watched as the two climbed into the red Volkswagen and drove away. Jeff opened his apartment door and went outside again. He stepped off the sidewalk and looked into Angie's window. She hadn't completely shut the blinds. He spied Lexi's large handbag and a laptop computer sitting on the kitchen table.

Jeff turned around and went back into the apartment he had just rented and closed the door behind him. Pulling his cellphone from his back pocket, he called his employer.

"She left her bag with the computer at Angie's apartment," Jeff explained when he had Ethan on the phone. He assumed the laptop belonged to Lexi.

"Where did she go?" Ethan asked.

"I overheard them say something about the mall."

"Did they both go?"

"Yes, they left in Angie's car."

"Good job, J.B. Call me the minute they get back."

"Yes, sir, I will."

Jeff took a few minutes to look around the rented apartment. It was one bedroom, sparsely furnished, with a tattered Naugahyde sofa and recliner, and a particleboard coffee table and end table in the living room. Smaller than Angie's unit, there wasn't room for a dining room table. A breakfast bar, separating the tiny kitchen from the living room provided dining space.

It seemed clean enough, but the furniture was worn and outdated. There was something a little depressing about the unit. He assumed Beaumont would expect him to sleep here. But for how long? Walking into the small bedroom, he pulled back the bedspread and discovered there weren't any sheets on the mattress.

He had left his purchase from the electronic store in the trunk of his car. Before the girls returned, he decided he had better make a quick trip to his own apartment and pack an overnight bag. Maybe he would also stop at the store and pick up some beer and a few groceries.

Giving the depressing little abode a final glance, he turned off the overhead light and exited the front door, locking it behind him.

On the way to his apartment, he asked himself if perhaps this was a good time to start looking for a new job. It was always better to find a new position before losing a job. He didn't have a terrific feeling about the assignment. He cursed himself for getting sucked in, yet he wasn't sure how he might have avoided it.

Back at his own apartment, he stayed longer than he had intended. He took a shower, happy to wash away the hours of travel. Instead of shaving off his stubble, he decided this was a good time to grow a beard. He would return to his clean-shaven former self when this assignment ended.

He grabbed something to eat before packing his overnight bag. Jeff didn't see a reason to rush back to the Hillcrest complex, considering the girls had gone to the mall. Women he knew could spend hours shopping. Several hours later, he reluctantly picked up his suitcase and left his apartment to fulfill his assignment.

CHAPTER FOUR

On the drive back to the Hillcrest Apartments, Jeff spied the red Volkswagen. He wasn't positive it was Angie's car—parked in front of a Salvation Army thrift store, several miles from the mall.

Jeff drove into the parking lot, pulled into a space several cars away from the VW, and turned off his ignition. He was about to get out of his vehicle and have a closer look at the license plate on the red car when the front door to the Salvation Army store opened, and out walked Angie and Lexi, carrying several plastic bags filled with clothes.

He knew they were clothes because Lexi tripped when stepping off the sidewalk, dropping the bag to the pavement. In her haste to come to her friend's aid, Angie dropped the bags she carried. Second hand clothing littered the pavement. The two girls quickly scooped up the merchandise and shoved it back in the plastic bags.

Before they reached their car, he turned on his ignition and drove out of the parking lot, heading back to the apartment complex before the two young women.

After parking at the Hillcrest Apartments, Jeff opened his trunk to retrieve his overnight bag and groceries. With the overnight bag hanging from a strap over his right shoulder and his arms filled with two grocery sacks, Jeff looked at the remaining bag in his trunk. In held the surveillance equipment he had purchased earlier that day.

"Shit," Jeff said aloud. "Sorry Beaumont, I'll keep an eye on her for you, but I'll be damned if I'll invade her privacy like that." Shifting the sacks in his arm, he awkwardly shut the trunk and walked to the rented unit.

In the apartment, Jeff left the front window open but the blinds closed. It was thirty minutes later before the girls returned to the apartment. When he heard them walking by the window he peeked out through the blinds and noticed that Angie was carrying a pizza box. After they went into Angie's unit, he called Beaumont to tell him it looked as if the girls would be at the apartment for a while.

Jeff grabbed a can a beer from a six-pack he had

put in the refrigerator earlier and sat on the couch, trying to figure out what he was going to do about finding a new job.

"Okay, you were right Lexi. You can get some cute stuff at the Salvation Army," Angie said after coming into the apartment. She placed the pizza box on the kitchen counter, then grabbed a roll of paper towels and set it next to the food before washing her hands in the kitchen sink.

Lexi dumped the sacks she had been carrying onto the couch and started pulling items from the bags, inspecting each article of clothing. "I know, really. Look at all the clothes I got, for less than fifty bucks. Quite a score. But I need to wash this stuff before I wear it."

"Yeah, I noticed, it smells kinda funny. I'll take you down to the laundry room when we're done eating."

After looking at her purchases for a moment, Lexi scooped up the clothes and shoved them back in the bags. Leaving them on the couch, she walked to the kitchen sink and washed her hands for dinner.

"Looks like someone moved into the vacant apartment across the way. I noticed the window was open and the blinds shut," Angie commented as she opened the pizza box and picked up a slice of the pie, using a piece of paper towel as a plate.

"I noticed that, too. I was going to mention it, but I had a feeling someone was watching us when we walked by the window."

"That's a little creepy."

"I wonder who our new neighbors are."

"I never heard anyone move in. It's a furnished unit, like this one, but you'd think we would've heard them bring in boxes or something."

"I guess they moved in when we were shopping."

"Speaking of shopping... you still don't have anything nice to wear on a job interview," Angie reminded.

"I just didn't like anything they had at the mall. But at least I got my underwear!"

Thirty minutes later, after they had finished eating; a knock came at the door. Angie tossed some trash in the can under the kitchen sink and peeked out the window before answering it.

"It's the cops," Angie said.

"Really? I wonder what they want."

"I don't know." Angie shrugged and then went to open the door. She came face to face with two uniformed officers.

"We're looking for Lexi Beaumont and understand she's here," one officer said.

"I'm Lexi. What's this about?" Lexi stepped up to the door while Angie moved to the side.

"An Ethan Beaumont has filed a complaint against you," the second officer explained.

"My grandfather? What are you talking about?"

"It involves the theft of a laptop computer, camera, and cellphone."

Lexi started to laugh. She couldn't help it. While she had expected her grandfather to do something, she had never expected this.

"So, are you telling me you're going to throw me in jail over birthday gifts my grandfather gave me—which, apparently, he is now ungiving me? Really? You're wasting tax payer's dollars over this?"

"We don't know anything about birthday gifts," the first officer said tersely. "But we have to follow up on this complaint, and if the serial numbers match the receipts Mr. Beaumont has given us, to show proof of ownership, then you have a problem. The courts can sort out any claims you have on the property."

"Really? He wants to have me thrown in jail on this trumped-up charge?" Lexi found herself getting angry.

"Of course," the second officer chimed in, "if you say this is just a misunderstanding and give Mr. Beaumont his property back, he has agreed to drop all charges."

"Fine!" Lexi shouted. She turned around, marched to the kitchen table, and opened her leather bag and pulled out the camera and cellphone.

Roughly snatching the laptop computer from the table, she took all three items to the officers, who continued to stand in the doorway.

"I expect some sort of receipt. I don't trust that old man, and I want some proof you took *his* property."

After the police officers left, Lexi slammed the apartment door and shouted, "He sent the cops after me? What is wrong with that man?"

"He's a prick. We always knew that. Just didn't know the extent of his prickiness."

"Ah, hell," Lexi chuckled, letting the anger subside. "The computer was four years old anyway; that's a fricking dinosaur."

"True, you needed a new one," Angie agreed. She grabbed a bottle of wine from the refrigerator, which had been open the night before. She pulled off its stopper and poured them each a glass of Chablis.

"But it does make me sick to lose my Adobe software."

"Yeah, that does suck." Angie handed Lexi a glass of wine. The two friends went to the couch and sat down, propping their bare feet on the coffee table.

"I will also miss my camera. That was a nice camera." Lexi took a sip of wine.

"You can use one of mine until you can get a new one."

"Thanks, Angie, but you need those for your business."

"I wouldn't make that offer to just anyone. I know how you treat cameras. The offer stays open."

"Thanks. You're a good friend." Lexi took another sip of wine. "I won't miss the cellphone."

"No kidding, since your grandfather was the only one you ever called on that!" Angie laughed.

"As much as I hate losing my software, it is liberating knowing he's out of my life."

"Now what?"

"Well, I guess I need to get a new computer. Maybe I can't afford another Mac right now, but I need to get something."

"Lexi, how much do you have in your savings?"

"A little under $15,000. I've been putting my microstock money directly in my savings each month and the same for any side jobs I did. But until I can replace my computer and my software, I won't be able to do any freelance work."

"You have enough money to replace your equipment."

"I know, but I'm a little nervous about dipping into my nest egg until I have a regular job lined up. Now that I think about it, I no longer have medical insurance. Grandfather always paid for it. I suppose I could marry Jerome Peters. I bet he'll pay for my insurance."

"Oh, gross!" Both girls laughed.

JEFF GRABBED ANOTHER BEER FROM THE REFRIGERATOR, returned to the couch, and sat down. He had managed to hear the entire conversation between the police officers and Lexi Beaumont through the open window. He wondered how far Ethan Beaumont planned to take this thing. It was obvious Lexi wouldn't be rushing back to her grandfather in the near future, if ever.

So far, the Lexi Beaumont he was seeing didn't match the picture her grandfather portrayed. When leaving the Beaumont house earlier that day, he had run into the housekeeper. She had seemed a little upset and confided in Jeff that their boss instructed her to box up all Lexi's belongings and throw them out if she didn't return within a specific timeframe. Apparently, Lexi Beaumont left her grandfather's house with only her handbag.

If what the housekeeper told him were true, that would explain the shopping trip to the Salvation Army. *Would a spoiled fashion diva replenish her wardrobe at a thrift store?* He wondered. The way Beaumont described his granddaughter, she was not a discount shopper.

Jeff began wondering how truthful Beaumont had been regarding the situation with Lexi. Had she once agreed to marry Jerome Peters or was that Beaumont's fantasy? Was the old man seriously worried about someone taking advantage of Lexi, or was he trying to manipulate the girl? Considering how she talked to the police officers, she certainly didn't seem like someone who was easily intimidated or manipulated.

For a brief moment, Jeff considered calling his boss and telling the man to shove the spy assignment. But when he realized that would only mean the loss of his job, and Beaumont would hire someone else to watch Lexi—someone who would willingly install the invasive spy equipment—he reconsidered.

While pondering his options, his cellphone began to ring. Setting the beer on the coffee table, he picked up the phone and looked to see who was calling. It was Beaumont.

"Hello," Jeff answered.

"I understand the police were there. Were you able to hear what went on?"

"Yes. They told her if she handed over the items, she wouldn't be arrested."

"Was she upset?"

"Upset?"

"Did she cry, throw some sort of fit?"

"No, she didn't cry. She seemed annoyed. She asked for a receipt for the items, but other than that, she didn't seem particularly upset."

"Let's see how she feels in a couple of days. Keep an eye on her. I expect a daily report. If she does anything noteworthy, I want to know immediately."

"What about my other job?"

"Other job? This is your job for now. When I hired you, I explained you needed to be flexible, and do what needed to be done. Is there a problem?"

"No sir. No problem."

CHAPTER FIVE

If it hadn't been for his iPad, which he had wisely put in his overnight bag when preparing for this misadventure, he would have gone insane being cooped up in the dismal little apartment for over a week. Since he didn't have a television at the Hillcrest unit, he watched the videos he had downloaded for his flight to Europe, which he hadn't ever gotten around to viewing on the trip. The tablet was a 3G version, enabling him to surf the Internet and look for employment opportunities.

Fortunately, he had been able to supply Beaumont with significant tidbits each day, and thus far, had avoided another conversation regarding installing the surveillance equipment he had purchased. Beaumont brought it up once, but Jeff managed to come up with a plausible excuse as to why he hadn't done it yet.

The unseasonably warm January weather proved advantageous. When home, the girls kept their front window wide open to let in the fresh air. He doubted they knew how easily sound carried in the corridor of their complex. It seemed most of the residents were gone during the day, which meant the other apartments stayed closed up most of the time.

He learned Angie was a freelance photographer, and occasionally she would take Lexi along on a photo shoot to help. Lexi replaced her computer the day after the visit from the police officers, a tidbit he failed to share with Beaumont. By the conversation he overheard, it wasn't a Mac, nor did it have the software necessary for her to take on freelance jobs. He heard her discussing the possibility of downloading a trial version—which she could use free for thirty days— along with the fact that she had the money to purchase software. Apparently, Lexi Beaumont had a secret cash-stash her grandfather didn't know about. That was another tidbit he withheld from his employer.

Jeff still hadn't shaved, and by the end of the week, he doubted his own mother would recognize him. He had been a little concerned about coming face to face with Lexi, in case she eventually went back to her grandfather. As the days progressed, that didn't matter as much to him, since he was looking for another job. Yet, if he stayed with her grandfather, he doubted she would recognize his clean-cut version as the scruffy neighbor from the Hillcrest Apartments.

From the conversations he was overhearing, he knew Lexi was also actively looking for employment. By her tone, she sounded discouraged. Apparently, some companies who had indicated an interest in her prior to graduation now would not give her an interview. He knew Beaumont dealt with several of the larger marketing firms in the area and wondered if the old man was sabotaging his granddaughter's efforts.

On Sunday, nine days after Lexi's exile, Jeff pulled into the parking lot of the Hillcrest Apartment complex, returning from the grocery store. Dressed casually, wearing denims, sweatshirt, baseball cap, and dark sunglasses, he was just getting out of his car when Angie's VW pulled up next to him and parked. When he glanced down at the other end of the lot, where she normally parked, he noticed most of the spaces were full.

He silently lifted his sacks out of the trunk and listened to Lexi and Angie as they got out of their vehicle.

"Hello," Lexi greeted him as she shut the car door. Jeff gave a nod of greeting, then turned, and quietly made his way to his apartment.

"I think that's our new neighbor," Angie whispered. Lexi watched Jeff for a moment then lost interest, resuming the conversation they had started in the car.

"I'll never understand my grandfather and why he does the things he does," Lexi said as she and Angie walked on the sidewalk toward their unit. Jeff walked in the same direction, about five feet in front of them and listened carefully to their every word.

"I think it's pretty crappy he doesn't want you to find a job."

"Well, he can't control me if I'm financially independent. I always got the idea he never got over the fact my father went off on his own and married someone that didn't fit into Grandfather's plans."

"Like you marrying his creepy business partner?"

"Exactly. You know, Angie, after this business with my Grandfather and not having any luck getting a job interview, I just wish I could leave town. Move somewhere else. Start someplace fresh without dealing with all this bullshit."

"Well, where do you want to go? I'm game."

"What do you mean?"

"You know I'm renting the apartment month to month. It isn't like we can't just pick up and take off. I can do what I'm doing anywhere. I wouldn't mind a change."

"But where? Moving takes money. I have to be careful with my savings until I get settled." Silently, they each considered the possibilities.

Jeff had reached his apartment door and was

unlocking it when the girls arrived at their door. He was thankful he had left the front window open, which meant he could continue listening to their conversation without having to open it and make them suspicious.

After walking inside the apartment and closing the door behind him, he heard Angie say, "I know what we can do!"

"What?" Lexi asked. They paused outside their apartment door.

"Remember when I told you the other day about the snowbirds who rented Mom and Dad's house in Havasu each winter; that they had to cancel at the last minute because of a family emergency?"

"Yeah."

"Well, it was too late to find another renter, and I bet Mom and Dad would let us use the house. All we would need to do is pay for the utilities, and this time of year, we won't need the air conditioner so that shouldn't be a big deal. It'll be cheaper than staying here."

"I doubt I could find the kind of job I'm looking for in Lake Havasu City."

"I know that, but it would be a safe haven while you regroup, away from your meddling grandfather. There's no way he'll ever know where you went. You can go ahead and get that 30-day free version of the software, get some freelance stuff going. It's possible to live anywhere and do that. I love the weather in

Havasu this time of the year. Not really swimming weather, but we can get out, do some hiking, take some great photographs.

"Hell, Lexi, we haven't even been out of college for a month, and we should do something like this before you settle down in a job. Maybe you'll decide you want to join me in the ranks of the fulltime freelancer."

"I might as well; I'm not making any progress here."

When the girls went into the apartment, and shut the door behind them, Jeff could no longer hear their conversation. They didn't open their window. Yet, he didn't feel it was necessary to hear more. It looked as if his stint as private detective was about to end. If Lexi went to Lake Havasu City, he could go home to his own apartment and back to his regular job.

After putting his groceries away, he went into his bedroom to call Beaumont. Knowing how sound traveled, he felt it was easier to simply talk in the bedroom with the door closed, rather than shutting the front window every time he wanted privacy on the phone.

"What do you mean she's leaving town?" Beaumont asked after Jeff told him some of what he had overheard.

"Apparently, she's been having a hard time finding a job. She can't get any interviews." To that bit of news, Beaumont chuckled, as if he already knew.

"Angie offered to go with her, since she does freelance work."

"Where are they going?"

Jeff didn't answer immediately. There was only so much he was willing to tell his employer. If Lexi wanted to get away from her controlling grandfather, he felt she was entitled.

"I don't know, they never said," he lied.

"Then get that surveillance equipment installed immediately. I wanted you to do that, days ago. Barnett, if my granddaughter disappears, it's going to be your ass. Do you understand?"

"Yes, sir," Jeff answered, feeling sick inside.

When the phone conversation ended, Jeff fell back on the bed and looked up at the ceiling, questioning what he should do. If he didn't give Beaumont want he wanted, he was out of a job, and someone else would be spying on Lexi and Angie. He didn't know why he felt a sense of responsibility for the girl, but he did.

When Jeff finally went back into his living room, he peeked outside and noticed they had opened their window. Quietly, he sat inside the apartment, his eyes closed, listening and feeling like a jerk.

"They said yes!" Jeff heard Angie squeal from inside her apartment. "We can use the Havasu house!"

"Woohoo!" Lexi cheered. "When should we leave?"

"I told Mom I'd pick up the keys in the morning. Help me pack, and we can leave some of the boxes at their house. I don't really care about staying at this crummy apartment for the rest of the month."

Jeff picked up his cellphone and went into the bedroom, shutting the door behind him. Sitting on the edge of the bed, he considered his options before calling his employer. If he failed to give Beaumont what he wanted, he would be out of a job. He was fairly certain Beaumont would hire a professional to follow Lexi, someone who could easily track her to Havasu through Angie and would be willing to install invasive cameras in the girls' house. Ever since he purchased the surveillance cameras, Jeff couldn't stop thinking of his own sister and how violated she would feel if some man installed hidden cameras in her apartment.

Another option was to tell Lexi what her grandfather was up to, but he had no idea how she would react. If Lexi stormed to her grandfather in outrage, he would undoubtedly find himself in the unemployment line by morning.

There was a chance Beaumont would want Jeff to continue the surveillance in Havasu. If that were the case, it would give Jeff time to find another job while still collecting a paycheck.

"Lake Havasu City?" Beaumont shouted after Jeff

told him where Lexi was going. "Isn't that where they have the London Bridge?"

"Yes, sir. I looked it up online before calling you. It's located on the border of Arizona and California, on a portion of the Colorado River."

"Spring breakers. I remember now. I saw a travel show about it. It's where all those wild college kids go on spring break."

"I believe that's around Easter, sir. From what I read, this time of year it's more a place for snowbirds."

"Snowbirds?"

"Snowbirds, winter visitors. Retirees who want to get out of the colder parts of the country and stay for a few months."

"What in the hell is she going to do there?"

"Apparently, Angie's parents have a house in Havasu that they normally rent to snowbirds. But for some reason, they didn't make it this year, so the place is vacant. I imagine they are house-sitting."

"Well, you know what this means, Barnett?"

"Um, no, sir. What?"

"You're going to Havasu."

"Excuse me?" Jeff smiled to himself.

"You heard me. Keep an eye on them, and let me know if there's been a change of plans. Meanwhile, I'll arrange a place for you to stay—someplace close to their house. It should be fairly easy to get their house's address, now that I know it belongs to Angie's parents."

"Are you sure you want me to go?"

"Certainly. Don't worry; I'll give you a generous expense account. At this point, I wouldn't feel comfortable having someone else take over." Beaumont paused a moment, as if considering something, then asked, "Has she seen you yet? You've been living across from her for over a week now. I don't know why I didn't consider that. If she's seen you, I'll have to get someone else."

"No, she hasn't seen me," he lied. Jeff was confident Lexi wouldn't recognize him once he shaved, but he didn't feel compelled to share that with his boss.

"Good. Let me know when they're planning to leave. When you get to Havasu, I expect you to find a way to meet her, become her friend. Keep tabs on her. I'll be damned if I'll let her spoil my plans."

CHAPTER SIX

January's brief heat spell ended, and the mid-morning temperatures hovered in the upper forties. Dark clouds hid the once-blue sky. It wasn't ideal weather for moving or traveling, but Lexi and Angie refused to postpone their hastily made plans. It was just starting to drizzle, which made them move faster when transporting the boxes from the apartment to the van they had borrowed from Angie's older brother. Since the apartment came furnished, they didn't have to worry about moving furniture.

They took most of the boxes to Angie's parents, as the Havasu house was fully furnished, and there was limited space in the Volkswagen. Jeff silently watched the girls from his apartment, peeking out through the blinds. He was certain they had no idea he was spying on them.

"One reason I'll be glad to leave is that creepy new neighbor," Lexi said as she shoved another box into the back of the van.

"You mean the guy with the beard?" Angie asked, as she glanced toward the apartment building.

"Yeah, what's up with that guy? He never seems to go anyplace. Doesn't he have a job? And it's creepy how he's been watching us all morning."

"I know what you mean. His blinds are always closed, yet he leaves his windows open, even when it's cold. And he's always peeking through his blinds, like we aren't supposed to know he's there. He's weird."

An hour later, Jeff watched as the landlord went into Angie's apartment with her, while Lexi waited in the van. Less than fifteen minutes later, the two exited the apartment, and Angie handed the landlord a set of keys. She walked to the van while the landlord locked the door to the apartment.

"They've moved out," Jeff told his employer on the phone a few minutes later.

"Are they on their way to Havasu?"

"From what I overheard, they're taking most of Angie's things to her parents to store, and then the two are heading to Havasu this afternoon. It's barely sprinkling now, but according to the weather reports, we're in for a heavy storm tomorrow. I checked the reports for Havasu, and it looks clear there. So, if they checked the weather forecast, I imagine they'll stick to their initial plans and leave today, before they run into some nastier weather along the way."

"When you check out of the apartment, I want you to stop by my house and switch cars. I had a new one brought over."

"What do you mean?"

"Your car's been parked in front of my granddaughter's apartment for over a week now. When you meet her in Havasu, you don't want her or her friend to recognize it. You're sure she hasn't seen you, right?"

"No, she hasn't seen me. She won't recognize me," Jeff promised, hoping that was true. He hadn't considered his car might be an issue down the way, but now that Beaumont mentioned it, he had to admit his employer had a point.

"After I get settled here, I'll go to my place and pack. I'll just leave my car at home and catch a taxi over to your house to pick up the other vehicle."

"Fine. I'll see you then."

LEXI FELL ASLEEP WITHIN AN HOUR AFTER LEAVING FOR Havasu. Angie listened to music as she drove from Southern California to Lake Havasu City, Arizona. The red VW bug was traveling east on Highway 40 and had just passed the Needles off-ramp when it hit a bump in the road, waking Lexi.

"Where are we?" Lexi asked sleepily, looking out the window. It was dark outside.

"Just passed Needles. We should be in Havasu within the hour. You've been sleeping for a couple of hours."

"I'm sorry, Angie. I should have taken a turn driving, or at least kept you company."

"Hey, don't worry about it. I figured you needed your rest. You've had a crazy few weeks."

Lexi sat up straighter in her seat and tried to stretch as best as she could in such a confined space. Once again settling back in the seat, she looked out the front window.

"I wonder when Grandfather will realize I left."

"Do you think you'll eventually call him?"

"I don't know. We've never been close. I always felt so guilty, like I needed to be grateful to him for taking me in, for paying for my education. But this thing about marrying Jerome Peters and if Grandfather really was sabotaging my efforts at finding a job… well, I just don't know what to think. I don't need someone in my life who is trying to manipulate and control me. I just wish I understood why my parents wanted me to live with him, especially considering Dad's relationship with my grandfather."

"Maybe it wasn't a matter of your parents appointing him as your guardian; maybe they just never had a will. They weren't that old when they</p>

died. Perhaps they just hadn't gotten around to writing a will and making those types of plans."

"No, there was a will. Of course, I never saw it, but the subject of the will was brought up when I asked my grandfather what happened to my parents' money. The ironic thing is that when I was a kid, I knew about my grandfather. I mean, I knew he and my father didn't have a relationship. I remember once… we drove down my grandfather's street, and Dad pointed out the estate. I was so impressed. It looked like this big old haunted mansion. Like something out of a movie. I wanted so bad to meet him."

"You mean, you hadn't met him back then?"

"No. I met Grandfather after my parents died. But I always wanted to meet him. I used to fantasize about it. I imagined he was this mysterious character who secretly missed me and wanted me in his life. All my friends had grandparents, but I never had one. Mom's parents died long before I was born, and so did Dad's mom."

"Wow, I bet you were disappointed when you finally met him. Not exactly what you pictured."

"I didn't understand that right away. Grandfather is an imposing figure, and he has always been a handsome man. I just never realized how ruthless he could be. Not until later. Later, I experienced guilt."

"Guilt? I don't understand, Lexi."

"For as long as I can recall, I had this secret fantasy about my mystery grandfather. After my parents died, I met with the judge in his chambers. I remember he asked me who I would rather live with, my grandfather or Joe and Carolyn Manning."

"Your parents' best friends?"

"Yes. I assume they probably came forward and asked to take me after my parents were killed."

"What did you say?"

"At the time, I don't think I fully understood the finality of my parents' death. But here the judge was offering up my long time fantasy of getting to know my grandfather, so I naturally said I wanted to live with him, even though I really didn't know him."

"When did you realize you picked the wrong guardian?"

"Not right away. I was still dealing with the loss of my parents, and Grandfather wasn't really around much. He was always away on business, and I was left with various servants. When he was home, I tried desperately to get his attention. I think I was about twelve when I realized the grandfather of my fantasies was nothing like the reality."

"Well, even if you had said you wanted to live with the Mannings, I bet the judge would have still picked your grandfather. Courts like to keep kids with family, and considering his money, that would probably influence the court."

"True. Plus the fact that, according to my grandfather, my parents selected him as guardian."

"Then why would the judge ask the question?"

"I figure the Mannings offered to take me in, and since they're old friends of my parents and I knew them, and didn't know my grandfather, the judge felt he needed to explore the options."

"Well, all that's in the past. If your grandfather thinks he can actually manipulate you into marrying his partner by taking away your car and computer, then he has a lot to learn about you!"

"Since I lost the computer anyway, I wish I would have grabbed the boxes in my closet before leaving my Grandfather's house. I don't think he could have really stopped me from taking them. But I didn't think about it until it was too late."

"Didn't you say it was mostly pictures you'd scanned anyway?"

"Yes, but still, there was some sentimental stuff I would have liked to have kept. But I'm grateful for the scanner and the fact I saved all my files online. Speaking of which, when sorting through my saved files, I came across something we need to try out."

"Try out?"

"I came across my dad's recipe for homemade hot fudge. It's awesome."

"Yum, hot fudge. You know me and chocolate!"

"It's Dad's own recipe. Mom once told me he took a fudge recipe from one of his grandmother's cookbooks and with some tweaking, came up with homemade hot fudge for ice cream. When I was growing up, Dad's homemade hot fudge sundaes were a special treat."

"So, how come you've never made them for me? You know how I love chocolate!"

"When we go grocery shopping, I'll buy the ingredients to make you one. Promise."

"What makes it different than the jars of hot fudge you can buy in the store?"

"Difference in flavor and texture. The longer you cook it, the thicker it gets. If cooked too long, it becomes caramel-like. That was Mom's favorite way to eat it. Sometimes she would overcook it on purpose, and when she poured it on the ice cream it would immediately harden, like chewy chocolate. Dad said she ruined it, but he always ate it all!" Lexi laughed at the memory. "It's important to stir it with a wooden spoon, so it doesn't sugar. It's cooked to softball stage."

"Softball?"

"That's when you drop a bit of the chocolate into a glass of cold water and the drop stays together, yet is still soft and flexible. If you remove it from the water, it flattens in your fingers."

"Sounds like a lot of work."

"My first year in the dorm, my roommate had a little portable microwave. I figured out how to cook hot fudge in it instead of on the stove. It actually worked out pretty well, and once I figured out the cooking time, it was fairly easy to whip up a batch. I could kick myself for not remembering how many minutes that was exactly."

"Microwave hot fudge… That sounds dangerous to me!"

"True. It's not terrific for the diet, that's for sure. And it can make a mess in the microwave. The stuff boils over if you try to nuke it in a bowl that's too small. I learned that mistake the hard way and really pissed my roommate off."

"Oh, there's the turnoff! We're almost there. Maybe another ten or fifteen minutes," Angie interrupted.

"Great. We'll be in Havasu before midnight."

Focusing her attention on the items in the baking section of the grocery store, Lexi failed to notice the young man pushing the shopping cart down the aisle. When he stopped next to her and spoke, she turned quickly in his direction. The first thing she noticed was the intense pair of blue eyes, glancing from her face down to her shopping cart and back to her eyes.

"Looks like a sugar rush. I think I want what you're having." He flashed a friendly smile, showing off straight white teeth. Lexi felt a blush coming on. She looked down into her shopping cart. It contained a carton of French vanilla ice cream, Hersey's unsweetened baking cocoa, sugar, butter, milk, and a can of sweetened whipped cream.

"Hot fudge sundaes," Lexi blurted out, though she had no idea why she felt compelled to explain her grocery list. It probably had something to do with the fact she was standing so close to an attractive young man, who was obviously flirting with her. It had been a while since someone this hot had cast a line in her direction.

He was about a half a head taller than she was, with broad shoulders and a husky, well-toned frame. Clean-shaven, he looked like someone who had just visited his hair stylist—not a barber—considering the trendy way the ends of his shortly cropped brown hair spiked along the top of his head. *Hunky* was the word that popped into Lexi's mind as she looked at him.

"I love hot fudge sundaes. My name is Jeff, by the way." Jeff held out his right hand in greeting. Without hesitation, Lexi reached out and accepted his gesture. He gave her hand a brief squeeze before releasing it.

She glanced into his cart. It contained a package of gourmet coffee, carton of whole milk, box of Cheerios, bag of mixed green salad, bottle of ranch dressing, loaf of wheat bread, jar of peanut butter, and a package containing three New York steaks.

"I'm rather partial to steak," Lexi countered.

"Then it's settled. I'll make dinner; and you bring dessert."

Lexi laughed at his invitation, yet immediately felt uncomfortable. The only times she had ever engaged a stranger in flirty banter had been on her college campus, with a fellow student. In the next moment, another shopping cart rammed hers. Steering the aggressive, grocery-laden cart was Angie.

"Did you get everything?" Angie asked before glancing at Jeff and looking him up and down. "Or are you picking up something a little extra?" She grinned mischievously.

"I've three steaks; you're welcome to join us." He flashed Angie a cheerful grin.

Angie and Lexi looked at each other; their eyes locked for a moment. Without uttering a word, Angie's expression seemed to ask, *Who is he?*

"Oh, he was just teasing me about giving me one of his steaks in exchange for a hot fudge sundae," Lexi answered the silent question, sounding somewhat embarrassed.

"I wasn't teasing," Jeff insisted. He looked at Angie and smiled. "Hi, I'm Jeff. I'm new to Lake Havasu."

"Hi, I'm Angie. You've obviously already met Lexi. We just arrived last night ourselves. You look a little young for a snowbird."

"So do you." Jeff chuckled.

"I thought guys normally picked up women in the produce section," Angie teased.

"I've heard that, too. But for some reason, a woman with ice cream, chocolate, and whipped cream in her cart just seemed more interesting than one shopping for vegetables."

Angie laughed before asking, "So, what brings you to Havasu? Vacationing or have you moved here fulltime?"

"A little vacation. How about you?" He glanced from Angie to Lexi, who was silently listening to the exchange.

"Not sure how long we intend to stay. It all depends on if we can find work."

"Really? What do you do?" Jeff asked.

"I'm a freelance photographer. Lexi is a graphic artist."

"It was nice meeting you, Jeff, but we should probably get going. The ice cream's starting to melt," Lexi interrupted.

"Did you get everything?" Angie asked.

"Oh, the vanilla!" Lexi turned around and scanned the shelf until she found what she was looking for. Snatching the package of vanilla extract, she tossed it in her cart.

"I still think dinner and a dessert is a good idea," Jeff told them.

"Wow, you're ambitious, picking up two women at once." Angie laughed.

Jeff smiled and Lexi shuffled nervously.

"Eating alone my first night in Havasu didn't sound appealing. And a hot fudge sundae for dessert sounded good." He gave Lexi a little wink. She studied his expression and couldn't decide if he was teasing or serious. The handsome stranger didn't seem threatening, but she knew looks could be deceiving.

"We'll have to take a rain check," Lexi finally answered with a smile. "You finished, Angie?"

"I'm done," Angie told her.

"Then rain check it is. It was nice to meet you ladies. Hope we run into each other again. Enjoy your stay in Havasu." Jeff gave them each a little nod and pushed his cart down the aisle, until he turned the corner out of the baking section and out of their sight.

"Wow, he was cute. He was sure checking you out," Angie told Lexi. They both looked down the aisle in the direction he had walked.

"He was kinda hot. Shamefully flirty." They both laughed at Lexi's appraisal.

"We really should've taken him up on that steak dinner," Angie teased as they started walking down the aisle, each pushing a shopping cart.

"With my luck he'd turn out to be some serial killer."

"Nah, he looked harmless. I have to say, Havasu has some great grocery stores!"

JEFF LOOKED IN HIS GROCERY CART, TRYING TO FIGURE

out what else he needed to buy. It was hard to concentrate. He had been watching Lexi and Angie for over a week, but until the encounter in the baking aisle, he had never looked in their eyes. What he saw in Lexi's eyes surprised him. Angie was an attractive young woman, but Lexi gave him pause.

He had felt the same way when he had first seen her portrait hanging in her grandfather's office, almost two years earlier. Something about the girl in the painting drew him in. At first, he fantasized about her, lingering by the portrait a few minutes each time he entered the room. He began asking questions, curious about the real-life woman. Unfortunately, the descriptions offered up by the grandfather shattered his fantasy, and lust for a woman he had never met turned into mild curiosity.

Initially, he regretted asking about her. It was like having a favorite pinup girl and then watching her interviewed on David Letterman, only to discover she severely lacked intelligence. Maybe some men found physically attractive airheads hot, he didn't.

Since watching Angie and Lexi, he had begun to realize Beaumont had misrepresented the granddaughter. The conversations Jeff had overheard didn't match Beaumont's assessment. He wondered why his employer would depict Lexi in such a negative light.

Upon meeting Lexi in person, Jeff realized the situation was now more complicated. This Lexi, the one he had met in the grocery store, was even more appealing than the girl in the portrait. While he wasn't in the position to start a relationship with any woman, considering his current job situation, he couldn't deny the attraction he felt for Ethan Beaumont's granddaughter.

A part of him resented Beaumont for putting him in this situation. *There would be some poetic justice if I got sexy Lexi in my bed on Beaumont's dime,* Jeff told himself.

Jeff checked out at the register and pushed his cart, now filled with bags of groceries, out to the borrowed car. While loading the sacks into the back of the vehicle, he noticed the red Volkswagen on the other side of the parking lot. The girls were getting into the car.

Smiling to himself, he wondered what Angie and Lexi would think when they realized he was staying just two doors away from their house. When Beaumont contacted the rental office requesting a specific area, they told him there were no available rentals in that neighborhood. After Beaumont explained what he was willing to pay, the real estate agent contacted a homeowner on that street, who lived fulltime in California and only used the house on weekends and during the summer. Considering what Beaumont was willing to pay, the homeowner had agreed to rent out the property.

Jeff hastily pushed his empty grocery cart to the

cart corral and hurried back to his car. If he timed it right, he would get back to the house Beaumont had rented before Angie and Lexi returned home.

***

"Angie, look. Is that the guy from the grocery store?"

Driving down their street, Angie slowed the car when Lexi pointed out the man in the driveway, two doors down from their house. The back hatch to his vehicle was up, and it appeared as if he was preparing to take something out of his car. She recognized him. He was indeed the man from the grocery store, who had flirted with Lexi.

Without conscious thought, she stopped the car in front of his driveway. Jeff turned in their direction and smiled. He gave them a little wave and then started walking toward the Volkswagen. Angie had thought there was something familiar about him when they met in the grocery store and wondered if this was why. Had she seen him in the neighborhood before?

"Did you ladies change your mind about the steak dinner, or are you just stalking me?" Jeff asked with a laugh when he reached the end of his driveway.

"We live over there," Lexi said quickly, feeling

suddenly embarrassed at the idea he would think they were following him.

"I was just teasing. I recognize your car; I saw it in your driveway earlier this morning. I just didn't realize it belonged to you," he lied. "So I guess this means we're neighbors."

"Wow, small world," Lexi commented, though she thought it seemed peculiar.

"I wasn't teasing about the invitation for a barbeque. Since we're neighbors, why don't you two come over tonight? There are three steaks in the package I bought. Of course, you'll have to bring dessert."

Lexi and Angie exchanged glances, as if silently eliciting the other's opinion. Smiling at each other, they both nodded before turning in Jeff's direction.

"Sure. Why not? When do you want us to come over?" Lexi asked.

"Around four-thirty. I'll get the barbecue started, and we can eat around five. But you have to bring hot fudge sundaes, or you don't make it past the door." He grinned mischievously. Both girls laughed.

"Deal, but I'll need to use your stove to make the hot fudge," Lexi told him.

"I think that can be arranged. See you at four-thirty."

"Do you want us to bring anything else?" Angie asked.

"No, I think I have everything."

"We'll see you then," Lexi called out.

Jeff gave them a wave, then turned and walked back to his car to unload his groceries. Angie pressed her foot against the gas pedal and drove a short distance down the street before turning in their driveway.

"Can you believe he practically lives next door?" Lexi asked.

Angie reached up and pushed the button on the remote control hanging on the visor. The garage door rolled open. She drove into the garage a few seconds later, parked the car, and turned off the engine, then closed the garage door behind her.

"Sort of strange. I guess it really is a small world. But you know, there's something familiar about that guy. I must have seen him around this neighborhood before."

"I doubt that, Angie. Didn't he say he was new to Havasu?"

"I know, but maybe that was just some pickup line."

"Funny, he seems a little familiar to me, too. But I can't place him. And this is my first time in Havasu."

CHAPTER EIGHT

Lexi filled a sack with all the necessary ingredients to make hot fudge sundaes. Not wanting to rummage through Jeff's kitchen, she added a pan, wooden spoon, measuring cup, and measuring spoons to the sack. The last items to add were the ice cream and whipped cream.

An hour earlier, Lexi had showered and shampooed. Using the hair dryer, she had tamed her naturally curly brunette hair. It fell into a smooth, slight flip over her shoulders. She slipped on a fresh pair of denims, which fit snuggly because they hadn't been worn since coming out of the dryer. For a top, she wore a cute pink cotton blouse she had picked up at the thrift store. On her feet, she wore a pair of flip-flops she had purchased on their way to Havasu. Glancing down at her feet, she wiggled her toes and admired her pedicure and blood-red nail polish.

Angie had dressed similarly. She wore her blond hair pulled up into a high ponytail. Instead of red polish, a garish shade of purple covered her toenails. Her artfully shredded jeans exposed hints of skin along her legs. While her blouse wasn't from the thrift shop, it did look as if she had pulled it from the rag bin. Angie never ironed her clothes, and Lexi resisted the temptation to suggest this might be one time to bring out the iron.

JEFF WAS PLEASED HOW FAST THINGS WERE PROGRESSING. It was sheer coincidence that he happened to spy the red Volkswagen parked in front of Albertson's when he went downtown earlier that day.

When he had first arrived at the rental, he had spied Angie's car parked in front of the house two doors down. After taking his luggage in the house, he had noticed the car was no longer there. Since the girls had obviously gone somewhere, he had seen no reason to stick around and had figured it was a good time to stock up on groceries. According to the real estate agent who had given him keys to the house, there were three grocery stores within close proximity to each other, all located on Lake Havasu City's main street.

The first grocery store he came to was Smith's, but he decided to head down McCulloch Boulevard and check out more of the town before shopping. As he made his way down the street, he had noticed the red Volkswagen in the Albertson's parking lot.

He thought his opening line to Lexi was lame, but that was the first thing that had popped into his head and out of his mouth. While he cringed at the memory of his inane contribution to the conversation in the baking aisle, the end result was far better than he expected, so he decided that sometimes lame worked.

Surprised that he was actually a little anxious about the impending dinner, he channeled his nervous energy into preparing for his guests. Not sure if they would be eating on the patio or in the dining room, he placed a stack of three dinner plates, three napkins, and silverware on the breakfast bar. He had rinsed the salad greens and put them in a bowl in the refrigerator to crisp.

Annoyed that he hadn't picked up some bread from the bakery section of Albertson's, he wondered if the girls would find the simple meal of steak and salad lacking. Rummaging through the pantry, he found an unopened box of rice pilaf. According to the date on the package, it was still within code. It called for butter, which he had also forgotten to purchase, but he had noticed some in the refrigerator, left there by the home's owner. He figured he would go ahead, use the items, and replace them later.

By the time Lexi and Angie arrived, steaks were

marinating in a pan on the counter, the salad was crisping in the refrigerator, and a pan of rice pilaf was simmering on the stove. Next to the dinner plates, he had set three forks, three steak knives, the bottle of ranch dressing, and a pair of salt and pepper shakers he had found in a kitchen cupboard. Lexi was carrying a sack, while Angie carried a bottle of wine.

"This place is nice," Lexi commented after Jeff opened the front door and welcomed her and Angie inside. The house boasted an open floor plan, tile floors, high ceilings, and pot shelves. Artificial cacti and clay pots decorated the high-placed shelves, and the home's overall décor was southwest, in shades of outdated mauve and sea-foam green.

"A little larger than I need," Jeff remarked, after shutting the front door and leading the girls into the kitchen. "But renting this late in the season, I was lucky to find it."

Curious, Angie walked out the backslider off the dining area to investigate the patio after handing Jeff the bottle of wine.

"I need to put the ice cream in the freezer and some of the other stuff in your refrigerator," Lexi explained, setting her sack on the kitchen counter.

"Certainly. Make yourself at home." Jeff watched her unpack the sack.

"I didn't bring bowls and spoons. I assume you have some."

"Sure. I noticed some bowls in the cupboard. That hot fudge looks like a lot of work. I'm starting to feel guilty."

"Hey, I'll gladly make hot fudge in exchange for steak," Lexi said cheerfully. She placed the ice cream in the freezer, then set the milk and butter in the refrigerator.

"Do you want to make it now?"

"No, we can make it after dinner. That way the fudge will be warm." Glancing around she asked, "Do you mind if I look around?"

"Here, I'll give you a tour."

"Why did you decide to come to Havasu on such short notice?" Lexi asked a few minutes later while Jeff gave her a private tour of the house. Angie was still outside on the back patio.

"I had some other plans that didn't work out. Havasu is known for great weather this time of year, so I called a couple of real estate agents to see if anything was available, and here I am," he lied. "How about you?"

"I graduated from college right before Christmas, and I'm still up in the air about my future. Angie's folks own the house we're staying at, and their renters cancelled at the last minute—so here we are."

"What about your family?"

"What do you mean?"

"Well, when I got out of college, my parents nagged me to come back to Portland—that's where

I'm from. They didn't understand that I needed to go where the jobs are. I wondered if your parents were pressuring you to come home. I don't imagine Havasu has lots of jobs for someone in your field."

"My parents are dead," she said quietly. Jeff felt like an ass for asking the question, especially when he already knew the answer. But that didn't stop him from asking the next one. "I'm sorry. Do you have any other family?"

"Just a grandfather, who isn't my favorite person at the moment."

"Oh, really?"

"Lexi, he has a spa! I am so jealous!" Angie's outburst disrupted their conversation. She had just walked back into the house and found Lexi and Jeff lingering in the hallway.

"You girls are welcome to use it. Swimsuits optional, of course," Jeff teased, and then quickly added, "I think I'll get those steaks on."

Lexi and Angie joined Jeff outside while he barbecued. Angie had opened the wine and poured them each a glass. The three chatted like old friends, and Jeff was surprised at how effortlessly the conversation flowed. He tried to share truthful tidbits about himself, but it was not always easy. They learned he worked for a corporation with a home office located in Southern California. When asked the company's name, he managed to change the subject and later mentioned he was looking for another job.

Of the two, Angie was more candid in her conversation, while Lexi was reserved. The topic of the grandfather came up one more time, and Angie expressed her opinion that the man was a controlling prick. Lexi changed the subject.

During dinner, Jeff came to understand why Angie, who was several inches taller than her friend, was so thin. She filled her plate with salad, using just a drop of dressing and didn't touch the rice. Instead of taking an entire steak, she cut off a small piece from one end, telling Jeff he could have the rest of her steak in the morning for breakfast.

Lexi was serious about liking steak and didn't offer any of hers to Jeff. She ate every last bite, even nibbling off the crispy bits from the meat's fatty end. Unlike Angie, she ate a helping of rice and a moderate portion of salad covered in ranch dressing. She wasn't overweight, nor was she thin. From Jeff's perspective, Lexi's curvy figure was perfect.

They ate their meal on the patio table, while watching Havasu's vibrant sunset color the western sky. It was a little chilly, but they all agreed it was too lovely an evening to eat indoors. They sat at the table for at least an hour after sunset before they cleared the dishes and went inside to make hot fudge.

Angie excused herself and told them she had to run back to her house for a few minutes to get her cellphone, which she had forgotten to bring with her. She left Jeff alone with her friend.

"So tell me, how does one make hot fudge?" Jeff asked, leaning against the counter next to the stove, watching Lexi. She seemed at ease in his kitchen.

"It's my dad's secret recipe. If I tell you, I'll have to kill you," she teased, as she set a pan on the stove.

"I won't tell, I promise." Jeff crossed his heart in mock seriousness.

"Okay, if you promise." Lexi grinned. "First, I melt five tablespoons of butter in a half cup of milk." With a dinner knife, Lexi cut off a chunk of butter from the cube and placed it in the pan. Next, she added a half of cup of milk. Setting the pan on a warm burner, she stirred the ingredients with a wooden spoon. She waited until the butter melted before adding the next ingredient.

"Now, I add a cup of sugar and three tablespoons of unsweetened baking cocoa. Dad's recipe actually calls for one baking square and four tablespoons of butter instead of five. But it's easier for me to use the powder cocoa." After measuring out the cocoa and sugar, she added it to the pan, stirring it with the spoon.

"It smells good," Jeff noted.

"I also add just a bit of salt." Lexi grabbed the saltshaker and added a dash to the mixture. "Now, I cook it until it gets to softball stage."

"I won't even ask what that means, but don't you have to add the vanilla?"

"I do that after it's done cooking."

Jeff watched as Lexi patiently stirred the mixture, which was now beginning to bubble up into a slow boil. She wore her dark hair parted to one side with no bangs, and a few strands were slipping out of place, into her eyes. He almost reached out and pushed back the stray tendrils, but Lexi beat him to it. Her skin was flawless, and he wondered briefly if it felt as smooth and soft as it looked. Tucking the tips of his fingers into the back of his pants pockets, he reminded himself to keep his hands to himself.

"So, you said this was your dad's recipe?"

"Yeah, my dad loved to cook. And he also had a sweet tooth." Lexi smiled at the memory.

"I'm sorry about your parents. How long have they been gone?"

"They were killed in a car accident when I was ten. I went to live with my grandfather."

"The one Angie is so fond of?"

"Yep." Lexi smiled and didn't seem particularly uncomfortable with the topic, so he continued.

"So, what's wrong with him, or shouldn't I ask?"

"Well, let's see. When I got back from college, he told me he expected me to marry his business partner."

"Was the business partner your boyfriend?"

"Hell no! I've known the man since I went to live with my grandfather, but I really don't know him. We've never even had a real conversation that I can recall. Although, he does have a habit of accidently copping a feel whenever I have the misfortune to be in the same room with him, and no one is looking in our direction. I have to give the guy credit; he's perfected the skill."

"Sounds like a jerk. Why would your grandfather want you to marry him?"

"There's only one reason my grandfather does anything: if it is good for his company. I basically told him to shove it, and he took away my car, computer, phone, clothes, and all the personal belongings at his house, which happened to be pretty much everything I owned." Instead of sounding devastated when telling the story, she seemed mildly amused.

"That's sucks. But you don't seem that upset."

Lexi shrugged and then said, "Well, he did pay for my education, and I don't have an outstanding college loan, so that's cool. He bought me the car and computer, so I suppose he has the right to take them back if he wants. I just wish he would stay out of my business. Interviews that were promised to me from contacts I had in the industry suddenly dried up after I moved out of my grandfather's house."

"Your grandfather sabotaged your efforts to find a job?"

"I'm pretty sure. It wouldn't surprise me."

"Does he know you've moved to Havasu?"

"Nope." Lexi turned off the stove and moved the pan off the burner. She added a half-teaspoon of vanilla extract to the mixture.

"It's done?"

"Looks like it. I can tell by consistency. It's a smooth color, no speckles. I used to test it by dropping some in cold water. If it forms a ball, it's done. But I've made it often enough that I can usually tell by just looking at it."

"Do we get to eat it now?" Jeff sounded like an eager child.

"In a few minutes. It should cool a bit, or it'll just melt the ice cream."

"It does smell good."

They chatted for a few more minutes and then grew silent, waiting for the hot fudge to cool. Jeff considered what she had said regarding her grandfather. He had always known his boss could be a bastard, but he had never realized to what extent.

Jeff thought about the boxes he had put in the master bedroom closet. He had forgotten about them when giving Lexi the tour. He was grateful her curiosity about the house didn't extend to the master bedroom closet. The boxes belonged to her, and it would prove awkward if she stumbled upon them.

When picking up the car at her grandfather's, he had again run into the housekeeper, who had confided in him that she had failed to throw away Lexi's things and was afraid her boss would find them and fire her. She didn't have the heart to throw out the girl's belongings. Jeff had offered to return them to Lexi and promised to keep the housekeeper's secret. He wasn't sure how or when he would give her the boxes, because he didn't want her to know about his connection to her grandfather.

Jeff watched as Lexi dipped the tip of her right index finger into the warm hot fudge. She started to bring a taste of chocolate to her mouth when Jeff reached out and snatched her hand, pulling her chocolate-covered fingertip to his lips.

Lexi's green eyes widened as she looked up into Jeff's intent gaze. His eyes never left hers. Deliberately, he brought her finger into his mouth and gently sucked off the sweet taste of chocolate. The tip of his tongue swirled around her finger as he held the digit in his moist mouth, reluctant to let it go.

CHAPTER NINE

"Damn, this is good," Jeff said as he spooned another bite of ice cream and fudge into his mouth.

"No kidding. It's a good thing this stuff isn't easier to make, or by the time Havasu's swimsuit weather hits, I'd be shopping for a one-piece with one of those little skirts." Angie laughed then took another bite.

The three sat outside under the stars, around the patio table, eating their hot fudge sundaes. Ten minutes earlier, Angie had returned from next door, just after Jeff finished licking the chocolate off Lexi's finger. Neither Lexi nor Jeff commented on the incident—each outwardly ignoring what had just happened.

"When I was in college, I figured out how to make it in the microwave. Now, that was quick."

"You need to market this stuff," Jeff told her.

"During my sophomore year of college, I seriously considered the idea. But not the actual fudge sauce. The thought of cooking and canning hot fudge sauce is way beyond my field of expertise or interest. I toyed with the idea of selling the mix, where the buyer could cook single servings in the microwave. Hot fudge on demand."

"Sounds like a great idea to me. I'd buy it," Jeff told her.

"I like that single serving idea," Angie added.

"The only problem is the butter and vanilla. I can use powdered milk, and powdered cocoa instead of the squares, but the customer would have to add the vanilla and butter. I would rather they just have to add water."

"I don't think it would be a problem to ask them to add the butter. Most cake mixes call for eggs and oil. And instead of liquid vanilla extract, use powdered vanilla," Angie suggested.

"They make powdered vanilla?" Lexi asked, sounding surprised.

"Yeah, my mom uses it. She orders hers from Amazon."

"Amazon sells everything," Jeff said with a laugh. He set his empty bowl on the table after scraping out every last drop of ice cream and hot fudge.

"It would be kind of cool if I could do that. I would design some great labels; package the mix in mason jars." Lexi was intrigued with the idea. "I could use the money, and it shouldn't take much capital to get something like this going. Of course, I'm not even sure how the fudge will taste with the powdered vanilla."

"So, try making it with the powdered vanilla tomorrow. I'm sure we have some in the pantry with the spices. Mom always keeps the pantry stocked with basics for the renters, and there could be some vanilla there, unless the last renter used it all or took the bottle home."

"If you're making hot fudge sundaes tomorrow, you better invite me."

"You know, Jeff, there's some hot fudge left over from tonight," Lexi reminded.

"Well, there won't be for long!" He laughed.

"About tomorrow," Angie interrupted. "I was thinking about hitting the flower, bridal, and party shops for business leads. Maybe I'll even stop in and talk to the local chamber of commerce. I suppose I'll need to get a business license if I want to do some serious promoting, but I'll wait and see. I don't think you'll want to go with me so that'll leave you without a car. Do you want me to drop you anywhere? Maybe down at Rotary Park, or the beach on the Island side?"

"She can come with me," Jeff suggested before Lexi could answer.

"Go with you where?" Lexi asked curiously.

"This is my first time in Havasu. Thought I'd do a little sightseeing, maybe grab lunch out. I'd love to have the company; it'd be a lot more fun if you joined me."

"That would be great, Jeff! Thanks," Angie answered for her friend.

"How about it, Lexi?" Jeff asked when she didn't reply.

"Okay," Lexi said hesitantly. "What time do you want to go?"

"We could leave around ten. Then stop some-where later for lunch."

"Sounds good," Lexi agreed. She smiled up at Jeff, who was watching her. When their gazes locked, she recalled how seductively his mouth had toyed with her finger. The memory made her blush.

LEXI SPENT THE NEXT MORNING ON THE COMPUTER, surfing the Internet for information on starting a business in Arizona. Initially, she assumed such a project would require a commercial kitchen, if she wished to stay within the confines of the law. To her surprise, Arizona's Home Baked and Confectionery Goods Program would allow her to prepare the hot fudge mix in her own kitchen—or in Lexi's case, in the rental's kitchen. She assumed she would need permission from Angie's parents, but she didn't think there would be a problem. After investigating what she needed to do, from a legal perspective, she was optimistic.

"I assumed there would be all kinds of hoops to jump through," Lexi said excitedly when Jeff picked her up later that morning. Angie had left the house early, and Lexi hadn't yet had the opportunity to share the information with her friend. She was excited to share it with someone, and Jeff was willing to listen.

"You wouldn't need a commercial kitchen? I was wondering about that."

"No, not for the hot fudge. Arizona has a program for some home-based food businesses. I'd just need to register with the state, which doesn't cost anything, according to the person I spoke to on the phone this morning. I'd need a local business license, which is only a hundred bucks for the first year. I'd also need to take the food handler's class from the county. It's a two-hour class and costs just twenty bucks."

"Sounds like you've checked everything out."

"It's a start. I would probably be wise to get some insurance, and I imagine I should do that if I want Angie's parents to let me use their kitchen. I don't think it'll be a big deal, because it's not like I'm actually cooking anything, and customers won't be coming to the house."

Jeff turned into the entrance of Rotary Park; a golf

course was on their right as they drove toward the lake.

"So this is Rotary Park?" Lexi asked. "Angie mentioned it, and I wondered what it was."

"I also did some online research this morning. Did you know they're having some big hot air balloon festival here this weekend?"

"Angie said something about it. I guess it's an annual thing. She's hoping to go up in one of the balloons and take some photographs."

"That'd be cool. You interested in going up in one?"

"No." Lexi cringed. "I have this thing about heights."

"I take it that it's not a good thing," Jeff teased. He pulled into a parking spot overlooking the beach and lake and turned off the engine.

"Not exactly. Last year, I went to the Grand Canyon with some friends, and it sorta freaked me out. I can't imagine how I would feel being up in a hot air balloon, looking down. It gives me the chills to think about it."

"If you want to hang out with me while Angie is up in a balloon, you can keep me company, and we can enjoy the festival from a safe place on the ground."

"You might be sick of me by then," Lexi teased.

Instead of responding with a playful quip, Jeff turned around to face her. They sat in the parked car.

"I seriously doubt that." He spoke in a low whisper. His gaze locked on Lexi, who was startled at his mood shift. "I rather enjoyed that little taste last night. I was hoping, after we got to know each other a little better, I might have another."

"Finger fetish?" Lexi wasn't sure why she said it. Perhaps it was because of his intent expression, as if he wanted to start nibbling his way down her body, starting with her lips, since that seemed to be where he was looking. The words just flew out of her mouth in an awkward attempt to lighten the mood. It must have worked, because in the next moment, Jeff broke into laughter.

"No, but yours was especially tasty," he said when he finally stopped laughing.

"It was the fudge." Lexi flashed him an impish grin.

"Maybe that's how you need to market the stuff."

"Sounds kinda unsanitary." Lexi wrinkled her nose at the thought.

"You did that brilliantly. I'm impressed, but somewhat disappointed." Jeff winked at her and opened the car door, getting out from the vehicle. Lexi grabbed her purse and got out from the car, closing the door behind her.

"Did what?" Lexi had no idea what he was talking about.

"Avoided my lame attempt at seduction." Jeff walked to the sidewalk that ran along the shore from

Rotary beach down the Bridgewater Channel and to the London Bridge. Lexi stayed in pace with him. It was a sunny morning with a clear, blue sky overhead, and several boats putted slowly through the channel.

"So, you're trying to seduce me? Kind of quick, doncha think?" Lexi teased.

"Perhaps. But I couldn't resist that sample last night, and since you didn't seem to object, I thought I'd make my intentions clear. After all, this is our second date."

"This is a date?"

"I plan to take you out for lunch," Jeff told her.

"And last night, with Angie there? That was our first date?"

"Very proper. Our first date was chaperoned."

"Interesting. Never really considered that a date."

"You let all your casual dinner companions suck your finger?"

"Damn, that sounds kinky!"

"No, sucking toes sounds kinky."

They both laughed.

"Stay away from my toes, you pervert." Lexi playfully shoved Jeff with her hip as they walked along the boardwalk toward the London Bridge. He managed to keep in step with her, in spite of the minor stumble from her shove.

"I won't make any promises," Jeff teased, then

added in a serious tone, "So you're really considering doing this hot fudge thing?"

"I'm thinking about it. It would be a way to earn a little money, which I could use right now."

"How would you market it?"

"Havasu has a Sunday swap meet. Angie told me about it last night, after we left your place. I was thinking about renting a booth, giving out samples of the fudge, and if people liked it, they could buy a jar of the mix. I'm pretty sure it would be exempt from sales tax because it's a food item, so I wouldn't have to mess with that."

"You could also sell it mail order, or put it in stores. It's really good. People love chocolate. Of course, you'd be wise to start with the swap meet first, see how people respond. It would be like test marketing the product."

"Plus, I could make a little money on the weekends."

"What about your graphic arts?"

"I never intended to look for a job in Havasu; always figured I would try the freelance thing like Angie. But to do that, I need to replace my software. I had everything I needed on my Mac, but I don't have that computer anymore. While I have the money to buy the software, I'm a little reluctant to take any more out of my savings account until I have something coming in."

"But you're going to need money to start the hot fudge business."

"True, but not as much as buying my software, and it might start generating some cash the first week I'm at the swap meet. Plus, I don't want to put all my eggs in one basket."

"What do you mean?"

"I'd feel more comfortable having a couple different types of income streams. I don't like depending on one thing. I'll probably go ahead and download the trial version of the software I need. That's normally a thirty-day free trial. I'll use it to design some labels and try to generate some free-lance jobs. Hopefully when the trial ends, I'll have some cash coming in and a few freelance customers, then I'll feel more comfortable making the purchase."

Walking along the channel, with the waterway on their left, they passed the London Bridge Resort on their right, with its castle-like towers attempting to make the transported bridge feel less out of place in its desert home. Up ahead, beyond the resort, five arches of the London Bridge stretched across the calm channel, connecting the Island to Lake Havasu's City's mainland. Before the city's founder, Robert McCulloch, purchased the bridge in 1968 from the City of London, there had been no island, just a peninsula. Initially purchased to attract attention to the then infant community, the bridge now provided the only roadway off and on the island.

When Lexi and Jeff reached the English Village, below the London Bridge, they browsed through some of the shops, and Jeff pointed out that her fudge mix might do well in such a venue if the packaging was attractive.

After exploring the English Village, they walked back to the car and drove to a restaurant for lunch. On the drive there, Lexi reflected on the morning by the London Bridge. If this was actually a date, as Jeff insisted, she couldn't recall any prior date she had ever been on where she had been the primary topic of the conversation.

CHAPTER TEN

"Where did Jeff take you to lunch?" Angie asked when Lexi returned home late that afternoon.

"Barley Brother's. Nice view of the bridge."

Angie was sitting at the breakfast bar, eating a carton of yogurt. Lexi walked around Angie and grabbed a glass from the overhead cabinet and proceeded to fix herself some iced tea.

"Oh yeah, been there a lot. What'd you have?"

"Cheese fondue."

"Oh, I'm jealous! I love their fondue. How about Jeff?"

"He had pizza." Lexi sat at the breakfast bar with Angie.

"Did he treat, or did you pay for your own?"

"According to him, it was a date. He paid."

"I wondered about that. Of course, going on a

date doesn't mean you can't split the bill. I thought he was interested in you."

"He asked me to go over there tonight and sit in the spa with him."

"With or without swimsuits?" Angie teased.

"He never said. But I'll be taking mine along."

"I'm hurt he didn't ask me," Angie feigned insult.

"You can come along if you want."

"I'm not really into threesomes."

"According to Jeff, you were our chaperone last night. You could be one tonight."

"Now I'm just insulted!" Angie grumbled with a frown.

Lexi laughed. "So, how did your day go? Any photo leads?"

"The people at Party Express were nice. I left them some business cards. At the other places I stopped, they were either with customers and I didn't want to interrupt, or the person I needed to talk to wasn't there.

"I stopped at the Chamber of Commerce office and happened to run into this guy who is going to have a balloon at the festival this weekend. We started chatting it up, and I showed him my portfolio. He agreed to take me up in exchange for a photo shoot."

"Sweet."

"I know. I'm so excited!" Angie grinned.

"I told Jeff you were trying to get someone to take you up, so he suggested we hang out."

"That's generous of him." Angie laughed. "Dinner last night, lunch today, spa tonight, and balloon festival this weekend. He's moving quick."

"He's just a nice guy," Lexi said with a shy smile, grinning to herself.

"Hot, too."

"True." Lexi grinned.

"So tell me, did you find out anything more about what he does? He didn't seem to want to talk about himself last night."

"I know, really. He was like that today. We talked a lot about my hot fudge idea, and he gave me suggestions. When I tried to ask him something about his job, he kept directing the conversation back to me, like he wanted to know everything about me."

"That's not normal for a guy to be that interested. They typically bring the conversation back to themselves. Maybe he's gay?"

"No, he isn't gay!" Lexi laughed.

"How do you know? Did you kiss him yet?"

"Not exactly."

"Oh, tell me exactly," Angie begged mischievously.

"Nothing to tell. I just know he's not gay," Lexi insisted.

"Why haven't you called?" Ethan Beaumont demanded. Jeff paced back and forth in the living room, the cellphone by his ear.

"I only got here early yesterday morning. There really is nothing to report."

"True. But I still expect you to call me every day. This isn't some paid vacation."

"I understand, but there really is nothing going on. I don't get the impression Lexi intends to stay here long. They're just using the house because the renter backed out, and Lexi hasn't found a job yet. I imagine she'll eventually need to go back to the city and start looking for work."

"So you've met her?"

"Yes, I ran into her at the grocery store and started up a conversation. When they found out we were neighbors, I asked them over for a barbeque. I get the impression this is nothing more than a little vacation for the girls."

"She can't afford a vacation!" Beaumont snapped. "How is she paying for food and other living expenses? Is she freeloading off her friend? Why doesn't that surprise me? But I can't imagine she'll get away with that for long."

"Apparently, she has money saved." The moment he said it, Jeff regretted sharing the information. But Beaumont's insistence that Lexi was nothing but a freeloader irritated him.

"That's impossible! I never allowed her to have a

job. And I sure as hell never gave her enough spending money that she could start stock piling it!"

The level of rage expressed surprised and angered Jeff.

"Continue to keep an eye on her, and find out what she has planned. I'm already wasting too much time on all this shit. That girl needs to get over this little rebellion of hers and get back here and do what's expected of her. Pay attention, and figure out someway to undermine this little spurt of financial independence she's flaunting. Find out where she banks, and if possible, get your hands on her checkbook. Draining her bank account would be one way to clip that girl's wings."

When Jeff hung up the phone ten minutes later, he stood in his living room, staring blankly at his cellphone. *What have I gotten myself into?* Before he could answer his own question, the doorbell rang.

"Hi, ready for some hot fudge?" Lexi said the moment he opened the door. She stood on his front porch holding a plastic grocery sack. She had changed her clothes since he had dropped her off two hours earlier. She now wore a flowered halter-top with her denims.

"I'm always ready for your hot fudge," Jeff said as he welcomed her into the house and closed the door.

"I wanted to test something, but Angie refuses to be my guinea pig. She says I'm trying to get her fat."

"So you want to fatten me up?" Jeff chuckled.

"Well, you don't have to eat it all. Just taste it. Plus, I'm curious about your microwave and how different it is from ours."

"Okay, test away," Jeff followed Lexi into the kitchen. There she unloaded the contents from her bag onto his counter. It included a mason jar filled with a powdered cocoa concoction, a cube of butter, a measuring tablespoon, and an 8-ounce, glass-measuring cup.

"Of course, we need to test this out on the ice cream I left over here last night. There is some left?"

"Yes, a little," Jeff said sheepishly. He was ashamed to admit he had consumed a large bowl that morning for breakfast with the leftover fudge from the night before.

Lexi went to the cupboard, took out a glass, and filled it with water from the refrigerator.

"This afternoon when I got home, I did some calculating to figure out a mix. There was powdered milk and powdered vanilla in the pantry, so I thought I'd experiment."

"So, that's the hot fudge mix in the mason jar?"

"Yes. It includes two cups of granulated sugar, one-third cup powdered milk, two teaspoons vanilla powder, and six tablespoons of Hershey's unsweetened cocoa. Oh, and a dash of salt. I shook it up really good in the jar to blend it."

"What now?"

"I figure a quarter cup of the sauce is a reasonable serving. First, I add one tablespoon of water to the glass." Lexi dipped the tablespoon into the glass of water she had gotten from the refrigerator, scooping up a spoonful. After adding the water to the glass-measuring cup, she cut off a tablespoon of butter and added it to the water.

"Is there some reason you took water from the fridge? Does it need to be cold?"

"No, but Angie told me Havasu's drinking water pretty much sucks, so most people have some sort of a filtration system. Chances are there's one on the drinking water that comes from your fridge. She also said most of the houses have soft water; that's why I don't want to use the water from your tap. It might give it a funny flavor."

"Okay. So, you add one tablespoon of butter and one tablespoon of drinking water to the glass. Now what?"

"I put it in the microwave for 40 seconds on high, to melt the butter." Lexi put the glass in the microwave over the stove and set the timer for forty seconds after closing the microwave's door. She continued to talk as she waited for the butter to melt.

"I learned something strange. Cooking time varies, depending on the cup I use."

"How so?"

"When the microwave turns off, I'll add two tablespoons of the mix and stir it with a knife, just to blend it. I don't want to splash the fudge mix all over the inside of the glass. Then I put it back in the microwave and cook it some more. In the microwave at our house, it cooks in 42 seconds if I use the 8-ounce glass. But if I use the 16-ounce glass, it takes a minute."

"Really? That's kind of strange."

"I know, right? Not sure how I can train my customers to use certain cups when cooking the sauce."

Lexi removed the glass from the microwave and added two tablespoons full of the mix to the butter and water mixture. Jeff watched as she cooked it for 42 more seconds in the microwave. After the microwave buzzed and turned off, Lexi waited five minutes before dishing up a small bowl of ice cream.

"You're mean, making me wait," Jeff teased.

"Boiling hot right out of the microwave will just melt your ice cream. Plus, the fudge will thicken a little bit as it sits."

Lexi poured the warm fudge over the dish of ice cream. She handed Jeff a spoon and took one herself. They each took a bite.

"Tastes just like the fudge from last night, just a little thinner. It's really good." Jeff took another bite.

"It was thicker in our microwave. Cooking it a couple seconds longer would probably thicken this up."

"You know," Jeff continued to eat the hot fudge

sundae as he talked, taking the bowl from Lexi. "It still tastes amazing, even if it's thinner than the hot fudge from last night. It's no different than regular chocolate sauce in consistency. I think there would be a way to teach the consumer, so they can fiddle with it and get the ideal consistency with their microwave. And you never know; some people will like it thin, and others will want it thick."

"Well, it does get like caramel if you overcook it. But one thing I learned this afternoon, if you cook it too long in the microwave, the butter separates from the mixture and you end up with this hard chocolate ball, swimming in a pool of oily butter."

"That doesn't sound appetizing."

"No, it was kind of gross." Lexi laughed.

"Well, girl, I think you have a hit," Jeff said after he finished off the bowl. "Now what?"

"You think I should really do this?"

"Absolutely."

"Well, I guess the first thing is to talk to Angie's parents, to see if they have any objections. Then I need to take the food handler's class, buy a business license, and register with the state," Lexi said excitedly, then she seemed to remember something and her enthusiasm dissolved.

"What's wrong, Lexi? I think this is a great idea."

"I seriously need to think about buying a car. I really hate doing that; it's going to wipe out my savings. But I can't really expect Angie to let me use the bug all the time, considering she's trying to get some photography jobs lined up, and she'll need it. But buying a car just for the hot fudge business sort of defeats my original purpose of generating income with minimal expense. I'd thought of getting a scooter before, but that really would not be practical for the hot fudge business."

"For now, let me be your taxi. We'll figure something out."

"I can't ask that of you."

"Why not? Sounds fun. It's my vacation, and I'd love to spend it helping you get your hot fudge empire up and running."

"That's sweet, but aren't you just going to be here for about a week?"

"When did I say that?"

"I guess you never really said how long you were staying. I figure vacations are about a week or two."

"I rented the house through the month, and I might stay longer."

"You can do that?" Lexi frowned.

Jeff didn't answer immediately, trying to choose his words carefully.

"Well, I'm not totally on vacation—I mean I'm on vacation, but I brought some work with me. You know—the wonders of the Internet and all."

"Oh, you're telecommuting! What is it you exactly do, again?"

Jeff smiled because he knew he had skirted that question and hadn't told her.

"Boring corporate stuff—nothing terribly exciting. Helping you get a new business off the ground… well, it sounds like a nice change."

Lexi looked up into Jeff's blue eyes. He seemed sincere in his offer. "You mean that, don't you?"

"Absolutely."

Encouraged by Jeff's support, Lexi gathered up her hot fudge supplies, anxious to move forward with her new venture. But first, she needed to go home and have some dinner. Sampling fudge all afternoon had messed up her blood sugar levels, and she craved protein to counteract the effects of all that sugar.

Jeff walked her to the front door and outside. The moment they stepped onto the front porch, they froze for a few seconds, awed by the spectacular sunset painting the sky over Lake Havasu.

"Wow, that's gorgeous," Lexi exclaimed, then added, "Angie needs to come outside and take a picture of that." Varying shades of orange and pink painted the western sky.

"That was a pretty awesome sunset last night, too."

"I know. On the way here, Angie was telling me about Havasu sunsets. She swears no place in the world has better ones, and I'm starting to believe her. I don't know why I haven't come to Havasu before now. So far, I really like it."

"I'm enjoying this weather. According to the reports, it'll be up in the seventies this weekend for the Balloon Festival."

"Really? That's almost a thirty-degree jump in a week."

"That's what they say. So, are you coming back later to sit in the spa with me?"

"Sure. What time?"

"How about eight?"

"Sounds good."

"Is Angie coming?"

"Angie?"

"Sure. Tell her she's invited, too."

Lexi knew how a balloon felt when pricked. Deflated, she concealed her disappointment over the invitation extended to her friend. It wasn't that she begrudged Angie time in the spa. But she thought Jeff was serious when inferring their time together was more along the lines of a date than a casual get-together. Perhaps she had read too much into that encounter in the kitchen the night before.

With forced cheerfulness, she made her way back to the house she shared with Angie, carrying the plastic sack of hot fudge supplies.

Why did I invite Angie? Jeff cursed himself as he watched Lexi walk back to her house. It was a foolish question because he already knew the answer. Lexi Beaumont had been on his radar for two years. He had been immediately attracted to the woman in the portrait, although his interest had shifted when Ethan Beaumont discussed the actual person and described her as spoiled, pretty, and not especially bright—someone who would make a suitable trophy wife. That description was hardly in line with Jeff's ideal woman. Of course, it didn't mean he wouldn't want to have sex with her. It just meant he wouldn't be interested in pillow talk.

How he now felt about Lexi Beaumont was a bundle of contradictions. One moment, he wanted to protect her from Ethan Beaumont and the next, he just wanted to screw her and get the hell out of Havasu and find a new job. When analyzing the situation, Jeff asked himself why he was even staying in Havasu, playing this game. No matter how much he argued with himself, he always came to the same conclusion. He was not ready to walk away from her, nor did he understand what he wanted from her.

"Tell Jeff thanks for the invitation, but I'm going

to pass. I've been fighting a headache all afternoon, and I think I'll go to bed early."

Lexi and Angie sat at the kitchen table eating hamburgers Lexi had fried up for dinner.

"Anyway, I thought this was a date thing?"

Lexi shrugged in reply.

"You kind of like this guy, don't you?" Angie studied her friend's expression.

Lexi set the hamburger on her plate and looked up at Angie. "It's really strange. We just met yesterday morning, and it's like we're old friends. I've never felt this comfortable around a guy before."

"More than just friends?" Angie prodded.

"There's definitely an attraction. I thought it was mutual, but…" Lexi shrugged again.

"But what?"

"Don't take this wrong, but when he invited you… Well, it was like my stomach dropped. I was so disappointed."

Angie began to laugh. When she stopped laughing she said, "I suppose I should be insulted, but I totally get what you're saying. I like him, too. Of course, not like you. There's definitely some chemistry between you two. I saw sparks fly when we first met him at the grocery store. Who knows? Maybe it's one of those terribly romantic, love-at-first-sight things."

"I don't believe in love at first sight." Lexi picked up her hamburger and took another bite.

"Well, maybe not love. Maybe lust at first sight."

"Or perhaps he's really a psycho. Some serial killer stalker."

"He doesn't feel like the serial killer type," Angie said as she finished off her hamburger.

"And how many serial killers do you know?"

"Only one or two. I tell you what. I'll leave my bedroom window open tonight, and if he goes psycho on you, let out a good scream."

"Then you'll call the police?"

"No. I'll lock the door and start looking for a new roommate."

"I'M NOT SURE WHAT'S MORE IMPRESSIVE, THE SUNSETS or the stars," Lexi murmured, enjoying the soothing hot bath as well as the celestial view. Overhead, countless twinkling stars peppered the dark night sky. She had never seen so many stars. While the spa's water felt wonderful, she imagined it would feel even better if she had been bold enough to strip off her bikini and skinny dip with her new friend. Considering Jeff was wearing swimming trunks, she didn't imagine she would be so daring.

"They are pretty amazing. Strange to consider they've been there all along, just blocked out by city lights and smog."

"Now I understand why Angie doesn't want street lights in Havasu."

Before getting into the spa, the two had lingered in the kitchen after Jeff poured Lexi a glass of wine. When they each finished their second glass, Jeff had suggested they go out to the spa.

Lexi's third glass of wine sat on the rim of the tub, half-filled with cabernet. She picked it up and took a sip before setting it back on the fiberglass rim. Sitting across from Jeff in the spa, their legs stretched out under the warm water, Lexi resisted the temptation to dip her hand under the water beside her right hip and tickle his submerged foot.

"Thanks again for the wine," she said before taking another sip. Lexi felt supremely light-headed and relaxed. Silently, she considered shedding her annoying bikini top.

"You're welcome." Jeff leaned his head back, closing his eyes for a brief moment. He hadn't turned on the jets and was enjoying the luxury of silence while submerged in the hot bath. Without thought, he reached out with one hand and took hold of Lexi's right foot, giving it a gentle squeeze. The foot wiggled in response while Lexi drew up her knee, making it easier for Jeff to reach her foot.

"You ticklish?" he asked with a chuckle.

"A little."

Instead of tickling, Jeff gently massaged her still-submerged foot, his own eyes closed as he leaned back, totally relaxed.

"Oh, I didn't know a foot massage came with the spa treatment," Lexi cooed, clearly not offended by the foot rub. "I'm a sucker for a foot massage."

Jeff chuckled at her comment and then moved his hand to give her other foot the same treatment. She shifted her body slightly and bent her knees to give him better access.

It was dark on the back patio. The only illumination came from the golden sliver of the crescent moon and the star-filled night sky.

"You mentioned you were looking for a new job. Why?" Lexi asked, still wondering what he actually did.

"I've a master's in business, and this was the first job I got after I finished college. I work for a large manufacturing company. It's been interesting. Lots of traveling abroad. I'm the private assistant for one of the CEOs. I suppose, I'm more a glorified gofer. But, the pay's been good. I can't complain there."

"And you can telecommute with that type of job?"

"To some extent."

"Why do you want to find another job? I would imagine there'd be advancement opportunities within the company."

"It's complicated."

"I've always heard it's easier to find something

when you already have a job." After Lexi made that observation, she wondered why Jeff decided to come to Havasu alone. She also wondered why he chose this time to take a vacation, if he was serious about looking for new employment. Before she asked the questions, she remembered she was unemployed, yet chose to escape for a time to Havasu.

"What are your plans tomorrow?" Jeff asked, shifting the direction of the conversation.

"I was planning on working on my to-do list for my hot fudge project."

"A business plan?"

"I suppose; something like that."

"Do you and Angie have anything planned for the afternoon?"

"I think she's meeting with that balloon guy she met, to take some pictures. That's why I figured I'd just stay home and work on my business plan, as you call it. I won't have a car."

"Remember, I'll be your taxi."

"You're sweet."

"Not really."

"You aren't sweet?"

"I have ulterior motives."

Lexi felt Jeff's hand move from her foot to her ankle. Gripping the ankle, he gave it a little jerk, causing her to slide toward him through the hot water. Lexi let out a little scream that quickly turned into a laugh. Jeff caught hold of her shoulders, preventing her from falling backwards and hitting the edge of the spa.

To maintain her balance, her hands attempted to grab hold of his shoulders, but he quickly maneuvered her sideways, pulling her onto his lap, where he held her there with a steely grip.

"If I scream, Angie will hear. She has her window open," Lexi warned with a giggle.

Holding her with a bear hug, Jeff didn't seem overly concerned with the threat. "You can't scream if I cover your mouth," he whispered into her ear, pulling her tightly to him. Sitting on his lap, she could feel the pressure of his erection straining his trunks, against her bottom. Had she been so bold to remove her swimsuit prior to entering the spa, this position would be far more interesting, she thought to herself.

"And how do you imagine that possible? You have your hands full," she teased, her voice low and seductive as she leaned into him. Without hesitation, Jeff's lips found hers.

CHAPTER TWELVE

exi succumbed to the kiss; not even for a moment did she hesitate or attempt to pull away. Releasing his hold, Jeff repositioned her and she complied, as if instinctively knowing what he wanted. Now straddling his lap, she wrapped her arms around his neck and held him tightly, returning his kisses with eager enthusiasm.

Greedily exploring her mouth with his, Jeff slipped his hands to the center of her back and deftly unfastened her bikini top, tugging it from her. The bra top slid between their bodies, until her naked breasts pressed against his bare chest. Carelessly tossing the bikini top aside, Jeff slid his hands up and down her body, his thumbs rolling over the sides of her breasts, while she squirmed against his erection.

Whatever plans he'd had of seducing Lexi, Jeff

had put aside that night. Or so he thought. Had she simply been some casual hook-up from a bar, he'd have been more concerned with moving her to a venue with easier access to a condom. There was nothing casual about his feelings toward Lexi, yet he knew the chances of a relationship with her were impossible, considering his situation.

The kiss was not premeditated, and her response came as a complete surprise. The rational side of his brain was no longer in control of the situation; his body was on autopilot.

Lexi could not get close enough. She wanted more. Until he kissed her, she'd had no idea how much she craved human contact and intimacy. Losing herself in the moment, she paid little attention to the consequences that would follow when Jeff gently pulled her hips upward and slipped one hand between their bodies so he could open the fly to his trunks and release his penis. Nor did she object when he took hold of her bikini pants and widened one leg opening, giving him the access to what he sought.

Instead of pulling away, she pressed into his hardness, welcoming him into her body without hesitation. Jeff's hands moved to her bottom and guided her movements as she rode up and down on his hard shaft, frantically racing toward completion.

When they finally reached the end of the path, they did so together with violent intensity. Jeff wrapped his arms tightly around her, pulling her close as he buried his face between her breasts. Leaning her forehead against the top of his head, Lexi tried to steady her breathing. Their bodies remained locked together.

Closing her eyes tightly, she asked herself what she had just done. However, the question did not inspire her to pull away. A part of her was embarrassed, while another, more primal part wanted to relish the sensation of their bodies joined in such an intimate fashion.

They sat together for a few moments longer, neither of them speaking a word, when Jeff finally lifted her gently at the waist. His spent penis slipped from her body and he casually tucked it back into his trunks.

Now more embarrassed, Lexi moved away from Jeff and fished for her bathing suit top in the water, until she found it. Slipping the bikini top on, she finally spoke.

"Well, that was surprising," Lexi said somewhat dryly.

"It was a nice surprise, if somewhat imprudent." No longer thinking with his erection, Jeff silently cursed himself. He tried to remember what he had ever read about having sex in a spa. Did the heat kill the little swimmers, or had he just knocked up Ethan Beaumont's granddaughter? The very least he could have done was pull out, but no, it felt just too damn good being buried deep inside her. In spite of the fact that he was pissed with himself, just the memory was making him hard again. *Damn*, he thought.

"Imprudent... Yes, I have to agree. Unprotected sex isn't something I typically engage in. Please tell me you normally wear a raincoat?" Lexi felt a little odd speaking so bluntly, but considering she had just screwed a virtual stranger in his backyard, she felt it was a little late for modesty.

"Even if we're both healthy, unprotected sex has other side effects."

Lexi noted the way in which Jeff rubbed his forehead with his right thumb. While she knew it was insane to have unprotected sex with someone she had just met, she wasn't especially concerned about him giving her a disease. Lexi knew she should worry, but for some reason, she felt safe with Jeff. As she studied him, she realized he did not feel the same way.

"Don't worry," she finally told him. "I'm on the pill. I've been on it since high school."

Jeff glanced up at Lexi. He couldn't see her features clearly because of night's darkness.

"Irregular periods," she explained. "Not because I have some active sex life. Now I will ask the question again. Do you normally wear condoms? Do I need to go in and have blood tests?"

"No. I had some pretty extensive blood tests

before I went to Europe last month, and it's been all work and no play for me since before the trip."

"When you say no play, are you talking celibate?"

"Pretty much. And you?"

"I'm normally pretty boring."

"You could have fooled me." He reached out, took hold of her right arm, and pulled her toward him, until they were sitting side by side.

"So, what now?" Lexi asked.

"I think we've become closer friends," Jeff said with a chuckle.

Lexi smiled, but she didn't respond for a few minutes. "This is all very strange."

"How so, Lexi?"

"We just met yesterday."

"Do you regret what just happened?"

"Can I be perfectly honest with you?"

"Absolutely."

"No. Not at all. I suppose I should, but I don't."

Jeff smiled and pulled her closer, wrapping his arm around her. He kissed the top of her head as she leaned against him.

"I'm glad. But I'll confess, for a minute there, I was wondering if I was going to be handing out cigars in nine months."

Lexi didn't respond, yet she found that comment an interesting insight into his character. He could have just as easily said, *I was wondering if I was going to be driving you to the abortion clinic in a month.*

While Lexi refused to imagine this was some love-at-first-sight scenario, as Angie had suggested, neither did she believe it was a tawdry, one nightstand.

The air was chilly when they stepped out of the water a few minutes later. Earlier, Jeff had placed two large bath towels on a patio chair next to the spa. He wrapped one towel around Lexi and took the second one for himself. They hastily dried off and ran to the house, escaping the chilly night air.

Entering by the glass slider leading into the dining room, Jeff turned on the light. Facing Lexi, Jeff silently reached out and took the towel from her, letting it drop to the floor with his.

"What are you doing?" Lexi asked, as his gaze washed over her.

"I want to look at you, please. I didn't get to in the spa."

Instead of answering, she just stood there, watching him. She wore a wet pink bikini and the ends of her dark hair were damp from the spa. Lexi said nothing, but looked up into his eyes. Her skin was pale, having lost its tan months earlier.

"Some women," Jeff said, his voice silky and smooth as his gaze swept over her, "will never look as good in clothes as they do out of them." Without asking for her permission, he unfastened the bathing suit top she had just put back on minutes earlier. Freeing her full breasts, he tossed the bra top on the tile floor with the towels. Lexi blushed, but allowed him this inspection.

"You're beautiful," Jeff said, his voice a whisper. Ever so gently, he moved the back of his hand over the soft curve of her breasts.

"I need to go home," Lexi finally said.

"Spend the night with me."

"I have to go home. Angie is expecting me."

"Call her, tell her you're staying."

"I can't. She's already in bed. I don't want to wake her up. Anyway, this is moving too fast."

"Too fast?" Jeff chuckled, then wrapped his arms around her and pulled her to him. "I just want to do what we've already done, but this time in a bed."

"I need to think about all this."

"Women think too much." Jeff leaned toward her and brushed his lips over hers. Lexi allowed him the kiss before placing the palms of her hands against his shoulders and gently pushing him away.

"I need to go now," she told him.

"Okay. But how about I take you to lunch tomorrow?"

"That would be nice."

Jeff flashed a smile, kissed her nose, then reached down and picked up her bathing suit top from the tile floor and handed it to her. Ignoring the fact she was practically nude in his dining room, Lexi slipped the top on like it was the most natural thing in the world to do. She had worn a swimsuit cover-up to his house and had left it on one of the barstools before going outside to the spa. Grabbing the garment, she pulled it on over her head, covering her body. Slipping on her flip-flops, which she had left on the floor by the slider, she grabbed her keys from the counter.

"I wish you'd stay," Jeff said one more time.

Tempted, Lexi resisted the invitation.

LEXI COULD FEEL JEFF WATCHING HER FROM HIS FRONT porch as she walked back to her house. It was dark outside, but the starry night and crescent moon lit her way. Angie had left the porch light on, but the rest of the house was dark. As Lexi suspected, Angie had already gone to bed.

She showered quickly, dried off and climbed in between the bed sheets and pulled up the comforter. Angie was staying in the master bedroom on the other side of the house. The glow from a nightlight along the baseboard near the door cast a yellow shadow against the wall. Staring blankly at the ceiling, Lexi clutched the edge of the comforter.

What have I done? she asked herself. It seemed as if she had been in Havasu for weeks. How was it possible she had arrived less than 48 hours earlier? Yesterday morning, she had not even known who Jeff was. But already they'd shared a dinner, lunch, her dreams and sex. She'd had sex with the man, whom she had met only *yesterday*.

Holy shit, I don't even know his last name! Gripping the comforter tightly, she pulled it up over her head and groaned.

CHAPTER THIRTEEN

*L*exi rolled over in the bed and looked at the alarm clock on the nightstand. The digital face read 8:32. Sitting up, she combed her fingers through her hair and yawned. Getting from the bed, Lexi grabbed her robe from the foot of the mattress. Pulling the robe on her nude body, she staggered from the bedroom to the hallway, fumbling with one sleeve, which was inside out. Lexi wasn't a morning person.

In the kitchen, she found a note from Angie on the breakfast bar. Reading the note, she learned her friend had left early for the photo shoot and didn't know when she would return. Tossing the note back onto the counter, Lexi grabbed a coffee cup from the cupboard. Silently thanking Angie for making coffee that morning, she poured herself a cup and then added a splash of milk.

Sitting down at the breakfast bar, she took a sip of hot coffee and then she remembered, for the hundredth time since waking. Last night, she'd had sex with Jeff. Closing her eyes, she shook her head in disbelief. While she never considered herself a prude, she had certainly never been promiscuous. A few of her friends would see nothing scandalous about her behavior. Lexi wondered what Angie would think, though she wasn't sure she would tell her. It was just too embarrassing.

After coffee and a bowl of cereal, Lexi returned to the bedroom and got dressed. Since exile from her grandfather's house, her wardrobe was limited. These days, her normal attire consisted of denim jeans, a cotton shirt, and flip-flops. *I'll buy some more clothes when I actually start earning money*, she told herself.

The rest of the morning, she kept busy and didn't have time to dwell on her actions the night before. Her first order of business: write a to-do list. *Call Angie's parents, order vanilla, food handler's card, business license, register with the state, call insurance company, swap meet, mason jars, buy ingredients, design logo, Facebook page, name for fudge…*

She called Angie's father on the phone and obtained permission to use the rental to package her hot-fudge-on-demand mix. The next call was to an insurance company. She went online and ordered five pounds of Cooks Pure Vanilla Powder, the same brand Angie's mother had stocked in the pantry. Instead of ordering it from Amazon, she purchased the larger container directly from the company's website.

Online, she compared prices for sugar, cocoa, powdered milk, and glass jars. She found addresses for locations she needed to visit, and she surfed through some Havasu business Facebook pages for marketing ideas. Losing track of time, she forgot about Jeff's lunch invitation. It was around 12:30 p.m. when the doorbell rang.

"You ready to go to lunch?" Jeff asked when Lexi opened the door.

"Oh, I'm sorry. I totally forgot." Lexi nervously brushed one hand through her hair. She had just thrown on some clothes that morning and hadn't even bothered putting on makeup or fixing her hair.

Jeff's gaze washed over Lexi admiringly; he thought she looked perfect.

"Have you eaten yet?" he asked as he walked inside and looked around. It was his first time in their house.

"Not since about 9 o'clock. I had a bowl of cereal. But I've been busy."

He followed Lexi into the dining room. There he saw the pad of paper, etched with scribbly notes, and her cellphone sitting on the table. "Working on the hot fudge project?"

"Yes," Lexi said brightly. He seemed to share her interest, which fueled her enthusiasm.

"I got permission to use the house. The insurance was much less than I estimated. I ordered the vanilla, and I have a list of places I need to go."

"Then we better get at it. But lunch first."

"I can't expect to drag you all over town."

"Don't be silly. I want to," Jeff insisted.

"Well, at least let me buy the gas."

"No way. But I will expect frequent hot fudge sundaes." He grinned.

"Deal. Let me get ready, and we can go." She was suddenly hungry, and lunch did sound good.

"Where would you like to go for lunch?" Jeff asked when they got into his car fifteen minutes later.

"I don't really know Havasu."

"Neither do I. I suppose we could just drive downtown and see what they have."

"You know, I did see one place I'd like to try. I was surfing through the Facebook business pages, getting marketing ideas. I came across one for College Street Brewhouse & Pub. It's on College Drive, and that's where I need to go to register for the food hander's class. The pictures of their food looked good."

"You say a brewery? Hey, if it has beer, I'm in."

Twenty minutes later, Jeff and Lexi sat on the outdoor patio of the College Street Brewhouse and Pub, each sipping on a frosty glass of handcrafted beer while they waited for their lunch.

"I can't believe this weather," Jeff said.

"Feels a little beachy to me."

"I understand it can get pretty hot in the summer."

"Angie says she's been here when it's 120."

"Shit. No thanks."

"I don't know." Lexi shrugged. "According to Angie it sounds worse than it really is. Of course, when she's here in the summer she spends her time on the lake."

"You think you'll be here when summer rolls around?" Jeff asked.

"I don't know; I'll see how this hot fudge thing goes. Of course, it also depends on Angie. As far as the house is concerned, they never rent it during the summer months anyway, so it's not like we're in a hurry to leave. I think her parents are glad we're paying the utilities. How about you?"

"I don't know." He took a sip of beer. Looking into Lexi's eyes, he reached across the table and covered her hand with his. It was the first time he had made physical contact that day. He squeezed her hand briefly and then released it, moving his hand back to his side of the table.

"What?" Lexi asked.

"I just wanted to touch you."

Lexi blushed at his pronouncement.

"I don't know how long I'll be in Havasu, Lexi. I'm not in a hurry to leave, but I can't stay indefinitely. I need to find a job."

"I thought you had one?" she asked.

"I do. But like I told you before, I'm looking for something else. I spent the morning filling out some online applications and talking to a headhunter I've been working with. He's setting up a couple of online interviews for me."

"I couldn't even get a preliminary interview. My problem is that I was focusing on local companies. I don't know why, but I wanted to stay in that area. I realize now that it wasn't the best plan, especially not for my career." Lexi started to laugh.

"What's so funny?"

"You must think I'm really flaky. I've a degree in graphic design, and instead of looking for a job in my field, I'm going off in the opposite direction and planning to market my dad's fudge recipe!"

"Not at all. I think you're a survivor with an entrepreneurial spirit."

"Survivor? Why do you say that?"

"Oh, I don't know." Jeff shook his head absently. "Just something about you. You don't really have any family support, but here you are, tackling a new adventure and doing it your own way. I find that very inspiring."

Lexi blushed at his assessment. "That's a very sweet thing to say."

"Not sweet. The truth."

"Do you ever think about moving back to Portland?" Lexi asked, redirecting the conversation.

"My parents would love that, especially my mother. She hasn't been thrilled with my job."

"Why?"

"For one thing, I haven't had a Christmas at home since I started working for the company."

"Sounds like my grandfather."

"Excuse me?" Jeff frowned, wondering if he had said too much. When switching cars, Ethan Beaumont told Jeff to use his own name when in Havasu. There was no reason to fabricate an alias, because Beaumont had always referred to his assistant as J.B. Her comment made Jeff nervous, and he wondered if she might piece things together if he revealed too much. Unfortunately for Jeff, he wanted to be truthful with Lexi.

"He was never home for the holidays, either. I never spent a single Christmas with him. Even that first year, after my parents were killed, he was gone."

"Who did you spend Christmas with?"

"I stayed home with servants."

"I'm sorry, Lexi."

"Oh, don't be. I'm so over it; it was a long time ago. I would just like to someday understand why in the hell my parents had me go to him and not someone else."

"Was there anyone else?"

"I guess not." Lexi shrugged.

"So, what were those Christmases like, with the servants?" Jeff couldn't imagine spending Christmas not surrounded by his family. Growing up, love filled his home and Christmas was always for family. He couldn't help but feel a little guilty for missing the last two Christmases, especially when he considered Lexi's family situation.

"Actually, it wasn't too bad. For years, my grandfather had a housekeeper named Mrs. Parks, who was really very good to me. I always suspected that if it wasn't for her, there wouldn't have been presents under the Christmas tree. Hell, there probably wouldn't have been a tree."

"What happened to her?" He knew there was no Mrs. Parks working at the estate now.

"She died when I was a senior in high school. I came home one day and found her on the kitchen floor. She'd had a heart attack." Lexi was silent for a moment and then she smiled, as if she had moved beyond her momentary sadness.

"But that was ages ago, and Mrs. Parks lived a long life. According to the doctors, she didn't suffer. They doubted she could have been saved, even if someone had been there when it happened."

Once again, Jeff reached across the table and

placed his hand over Lexi's, giving it a reassuring squeeze. Lexi looked up into Jeff's eyes and wondered what he was thinking. His expression was so intent, so caring. *When was the last time a man looked at me as if he actually cared about me?* She did not date boys in high school. Her grandfather did not allow it. In college, she'd had two serious boyfriends—one in her freshman year, whom she had lost her virginity to and one during her junior year. Each relationship had ended the week after she brought the boy home to meet her grandfather.

CHAPTER FOURTEEN

By Thursday, colorful hot air balloons were already drifting over Lake Havasu. Jeff purchased tickets for the event, and Lexi agreed to go with him. While she could freely observe the hot air balloons from one of the public beaches, having tickets allowed them to enter the balloon field and enjoy the various concessions and events.

Jeff picked Lexi up early on Friday morning. The field was teeming with activities. Tethered balloon rides were available, but Jeff was unable to coax Lexi up for a ride. The four-day event included live entertainment, a kite show, skydivers, gymnastic demonstrations, and train rides for the kids.

On Sunday, Lexi and Jeff made time to stop at the Sunday swap meet to sign up for a booth. She was determined to move quickly with her hot fudge project.

Angie had made friends with a number of participants in the event, and the four-day weekend turned into a party of sorts that included Lexi and Jeff. It also meant Lexi and Jeff never seemed to have another opportunity to be alone with each other. At least, not in the same way as they had been in the spa.

When Tuesday rolled around, Lexi had a food handler's class to attend. Angie drove her to the class and picked her up when it was over. On Wednesday, her powdered vanilla arrived. She finally downloaded the free trial version of the graphic design software and started designing a logo and labels for the hot fudge, along with setting up a Facebook business page.

By Friday, she was in full production, with Jeff's help. Her goal was to sell two dozen jars of the hot fudge mix on Sunday, which she had decided to call *Walt's Hot Fudge on Demand*. Walt had been her father's name. The cost per jar of mix was five dollars, and she was planning to price them at twenty dollars each. This would net her $360, not including labor—if she sold all twenty-four jars. She based her price on what similar products sold for online.

Lexi began with sanitizing the mason jars in the dishwasher and making certain they were completely dry. Filling them with the ingredients went quickly, especially after Jeff came up with an efficient assembly line. When it came to mixing the ingredients, it got a little silly, with the two dancing around the kitchen, each holding a lidded jar filled with powdered mixture, shaking the glass containers like soundless maracas.

Jeff held a jar over his head, jiggling it back and forth, as he swung his hips, looking more ridiculous than sexy. Lexi did a little shimmy, holding her jar close to her body as she shook the powdered mix from one side to the other in the glass container. Jeff watched her dance, and they both began to laugh.

"At least we figured out a way to burn off those calories from all that fudge sampling!" Lexi laughed, no longer dancing as she tried to catch her breath. "Maybe we should have Angie tape us. We could add the video to the hot fudge's Facebook page."

"I don't think so." Jeff chuckled and set the jar on the counter. Reaching out, he took Lexi's jar from her and set it with his before pulling her into his arms. She went willingly and looked up into his blue eyes. Since the encounter in the spa, they'd stolen a few random kisses and held hands, yet there always seemed to be someone around. Until now.

"Spend the night with me," Jeff asked, holding her in his arms.

In reply, Lexi leaned her forehead against his right shoulder, as her arms wrapped around his waist. She had never felt as safe as she had in Jeff's arms. It no longer seemed strange to her that they'd had sex that night. It only seemed strange that they hadn't had it again.

"Okay," Lexi leaned back slightly and looked up into his face. "But don't forget we have a lot to do tomorrow to get ready for Sunday, so we have to actually sleep."

"We can sleep, *after*."

"*After?*" Lexi asked in a teasing tone.

"After I do all sorts of wicked things to your sweet body."

Angie arrived before Jeff had the opportunity to elaborate on what wicked things he had in mind. They finished packaging the mix and cleaned the kitchen while Angie sat at the breakfast bar, watching and chatting with her friends.

Instead of sticker labels, Lexi designed decorative tags printed on heavy stock paper. After using twine to attach a tag to each jar, she put the jars back in the cardboard boxes they'd originally come in.

Jeff announced he was running to the store to pick up something to barbecue for dinner and gave Lexi a quick kiss goodbye before leaving.

"He really is a nice guy," Angie said. "I also noticed he didn't invite me for dinner. Hmmm, a romantic dinner for two?"

"Actually, I'm spending the night at his house," Lexi said shyly.

"Really? Well it's about time. Wait a minute… Have you two… already?"

Lexi smiled in reply, not answering.

"So, what's the deal with you two? I haven't really heard him talk about leaving, but I know he mentioned looking for a job."

"He's had a couple online interviews. The way he talks, I really don't think he'll be returning to his old job."

"So, is this thing serious? I know you. You aren't someone who casually does sleepovers."

"We haven't talked about it. For one thing, it's way too soon. Hell, we haven't even known each other for two weeks. But there's definitely something there. I'll wait and see where he lands and how we're both feeling toward each other at the time. While it's premature to even think about moving in together, I would seriously consider moving where he settles—just to give us a chance, if we both are still feeling the same way. It isn't like I have any ties."

"Finding someone you really click with isn't easy. It sure seems to me that you two click. I love how supportive he is of you. It's like you have your own hunky cheerleader."

Lexi blushed. "Yeah, he makes me feel special. I like that he comes from a tight-knit family. He's really close to his mom and his sister."

"Well, guys who have healthy relationships with their mothers and sisters tend to be good to their women."

"I thought guys who were close with their mothers didn't do well in relationships."

"I said *healthy relationships*. There is a difference, Lexi."

"True."

"So, how are you planning to push this stuff at the swap meet?"

"Jeff came up with a great idea. He stopped at one of the local restaurants and talked them into selling him a couple sleeves of soufflé cups and lids."

"What's that?"

"It's those little plastic cups restaurants put salad dressing in. Disposable, and they have lids. I'm going to make up a batch of fudge and give out 2-ounce samples, each with a little wooden spoon. Jeff also got me some of those. The kind used in individual servings of ice cream."

"How will the fudge hold up?"

"We'll keep them in an ice chest, pass them out. They'll be all cold and fudgy. Jeff thinks tasting the fudge will sell it."

"I think you should hire Jeff to work for you, I hear he's looking for a job, and he seems to come up with some good ideas."

Lexi laughed, then said, "Trust me, I've thought about that. He's made this adventure so much fun. Even if it doesn't work out, I'm really enjoying myself. This is the most fun I've had in such a long time."

"I wanted to tell you I love the tags you designed. You're really talented, girl. Even without the free sample, I think your packaging alone could sell the product. Other than making the fudge, do you have anything else to do?"

"Not really. Jeff was a sweetheart and picked up a table and EZ-Up canopy for the swap meet when I was taking the food handlers class. They're over at his house. I practically had to twist his arm to let me pay for it. He finally accepted my money when I explained I needed to treat this venture profession- ally and keep track of all my expenses. I still need to get some business cards, but I went ahead and printed some when I was at Staples, using business card paper."

"Ouch. I bet that was expensive."

"It wasn't bad. I needed something fast. I also found some cute plastic jars online, much cheaper than the glass mason jars. I can see eventually using something like that if I start shipping the product. Not only would it be cheaper, but they wouldn't break."

"You're really getting into this thing."

"I guess I am." Lexi smiled.

"DID YOU GET HOLD OF HER CHECKBOOK? DEBIT CARD, something?" Ethan Beaumont asked. "It's been almost two weeks. She should've been home by now."

Sitting in the car in the Albertson's parking lot, Jeff held the cellphone to his ear as he listened to the ranting of his employer.

"I don't think she has that much money," he lied. "She really isn't spending any. I don't think it's costing her anything to live with Angie. She doesn't have a car, so it isn't like she has any expenses."

"The girl has to eat. Is she sponging off her friend?"

"I didn't say that." Jeff wanted to suggest that this endeavor was futile—it would be best if he simply came home and Ethan forgot about whatever plans he had for Lexi. But he didn't want to go home. He knew if Ethan suggested that, he would quit and stay with her. Yet, he wasn't sure how all that would work, since Ethan was paying for the house.

"Barnett, you have one week. Peters will be coming back from London sometime within the next two weeks, and I intend to have Lexi at home, waiting for him and prepared to accept his proposal. I'm not getting any younger, and when I die I want to know my company will eventually go to my great-grandchildren."

"But, sir, can't that still happen if Lexi marries someone else?"

"I don't want the company I built from the ground up to go to some loser my granddaughter picks if left to her own devices. You never met her only two boyfriends. They were losers. Fortunately, it didn't take much to buy them off and convince them to disappear. Peters already owns half of the company, and he's the only one I trust. I don't want to worry about my company when I'm gone."

When you're gone, you won't be here to worry, Jeff thought.

"One week, Barnett. If she isn't here by next Friday, come home, and I'll handle it myself. And when you do come home, drop the car off at the office and pick up your severance check."

Jeff sat in his car staring at the cellphone. At least now, he knew; if he didn't deliver Lexi, in one week he was officially out of a job. *I need to tell Lexi,* he told himself.

CHAPTER FIFTEEN

Standing under the showerhead, Lexi closed her eyes and enjoyed the steady pounding of the hot water as it pelted her back and ran down her body. Tipping her head back, she allowed the oncoming water to drench her hair. Stepping partially out of the steady stream, she opened her eyes and picked up a bar of soap from the small built-in shelf to her right. Giving her skin a thorough cleaning, she thought of the upcoming night with Jeff.

Remembering their scandalous moment in the spa made her tingle and smile. It had happened so quickly and spontaneously. She wondered if a preordained evening of intimacy would live up to that memory or fall flat and strain their relationship.

What is our relationship? Contemplating that question, she stood directly under the showerhead and rinsed her body before reaching for a bottle of shampoo.

Thirty minutes later, Lexi was in the bedroom, dressing for her evening with Jeff. Her hair was clean and dried, as was her body. Instead of jeans, she decided to wear a bright, floor-length cotton dress she had picked up at the thrift shop. Its fabric's sunny print pattern reminded her of summer and trips to the beach.

Giggling mischievously, she tossed her bra and panties aside. *No reason for underwear*, she thought. After rubbing moisturizer cream into her skin, she slipped on the dress. She liked the way it fit; it felt comfortable.

Alex normally slept in the nude and didn't imagine Jeff would mind if she did so at his house. Grabbing her robe and a change of clothes for the morning, she stuffed them into a small plastic grocery bag. In her purse, she put her makeup bag, hairbrush, and toothbrush.

After saying her goodbyes to Angie, she slipped on her flip-flops and headed to Jeff's, carrying her purse and makeshift overnight bag. It was a short walk. She knocked on the door but didn't wait for him to answer. It was unlocked, so she went inside.

"Hello!" Lexi called out.

"In the kitchen, Lexi!"

When walking through the dining room en route to the kitchen, Lexi tossed her two bags on the table and turned to face the breakfast bar. Jeff stood in the kitchen, on the other side of the counter, facing Lexi. He wasn't wearing a shirt. On the tile counter before him was a large tray holding bites-size pieces of food.

"What are you doing?" Lexi asked. Whatever he was doing, it looked interesting and tasty. Still standing in the dining room, she leaned against the edge of the counter and looked at the tray. It held a random array of finger foods. Strawberries, grapes, chunks of cheese, smoked salmon, neatly rolled deli meats, and hunks of bread filled the tray.

"I'm making dinner."

"I thought you were going to barbecue, but this looks more interesting." She reached for a berry, but he swatted her hand away. Giving him a pout, she pulled her hand back, but then reached out and successfully snatched a berry and quickly popped it in her mouth.

"Brat." Jeff chuckled. "When I got to the store, I changed my mind about a barbeque. Thought I'd do something a little different."

"Oh, I love salmon, almost as much as steak!"

"Keep your hands off the food or I'll have to punish you," Jeff said in mock seriousness.

"Now, that sounds kinda interesting. But where is the whipped cream for the strawberries?"

"Ah, whipped cream! Thanks for reminding me. There's also dipping sauce for the bread." Jeff walked to the refrigerator. She noticed he wore plaid pajama bottoms and his feet were bare. Lexi watched as he removed a small bowl from the refrigerator, filled with oil-based dipping sauce. He set it adjacent to the bread on the tray. Next, he took a can of whipped cream from the refrigerator and used it to fill a second bowl. That, he placed next to the strawberries.

"Hungry?" he asked before leaning over the counter to kiss her. She met him half way.

After the kiss, she said, "Yes, but are you going to swat my hand again?"

"Not your hand. Maybe your bottom." Grinning, he arched his brows.

"If I try to take any more food?"

"No, just for fun."

"Jeffery Barnett, I never took you for a bully!" Lexi feigned outrage.

"Hardly." Jeff gave her another quick kiss and then poured two classes of red wine. "Ready for dinner?"

"Where are we eating? Outside?"

"No. In bed."

"Really?" Lexi smiled at the idea.

"Grab the glasses, and I'll take the tray." Jeff tucked the wine bottle under his arm and grabbed the food.

With a wine glass in each hand, Lexi followed Jeff to his bedroom. She paused at the doorway, surprised at the effort he had obviously made when preparing for this evening. A dozen lit candles sat on the dresser, their wicks flickering. Aside from candle-light, the room's only illumination came from the adjoining master bath.

Noticing a hint of lavender as she walked into the room, she guessed some of the candles were scented. Jeff put the bottle of wine on a nightstand and set the tray in the center of the bed. He took the glasses from Lexi and set them on the nightstand.

The neatly turned down bed revealed powder-blue sheets under the sapphire-blue bedspread. Four plump pillows, each tucked into a powder-blue pillowcase, rested in two stacks at the headboard. Jeff sat on the edge of the mattress and gave it a little pat with his hand, gesturing for Lexi to join him.

"Clean sheets for my lady," he said as she sat next to him.

"Wow, clean sheets, too. I'm impressed." Lexi grinned, suddenly feeling shy.

"Don't worry; I don't plan to jump you… at least, not immediately. I thought it would be nice if we could just relax, talk a little; eat our dinner." Jeff stretched out on the bed and leaned against one stack of pillows, watching Lexi.

She stood up and moved around the mattress, then sat down again and stretched out next to Jeff after kicking off her flip-flops. The tray was between them as she leaned against the second pile of pillows.

"Are you planning to feed me grapes, or am I supposed to feed you?"

In response to Lexi's playful question, Jeff pulled a grape off its vine and popped it into Lexi's mouth. He turned briefly, took one of the glasses of wine from the nightstand, and handed it to her. She sipped the wine after eating the grape. Jeff reached for the second glass and took a sip.

"So, do you do this for all your women? I feel like I'm in one of those old Doris Day movies."

"You watch Doris Day?"

"Mrs. Parks, our housekeeper, would watch them with me when I was younger. She was a big Doris Day fan."

Lexi seemed reluctant to take any food so Jeff promised, "I won't swat your hand."

"Excuse me?"

"Go ahead, eat. Unless you want me to feed you."

"This is very sweet of you." Lexi took a piece of salmon.

"What can I say? I'm a sweet guy."

Lexi chuckled and then helped herself to some cheese.

"Assuming you didn't just watch Doris Day when you were a kid. What was your favorite non-Doris Day movie?" Jeff asked.

"That's easy. *Labyrinth*."

He laughed. "Damn, that's my sister's favorite, too. I liked it the first ten times I saw it, after that, not so much."

"That is an awesome movie. I know all the words to every song."

"You and my sister both. When you meet her you two can have a sing along."

"Meet her?"

"Am I moving too fast?"

"Considering the spa, I think fast is what we do."

"Any regrets?"

"If I did, I wouldn't be here."

"I'm glad you're here."

Lexi had just picked up a piece of cheese, and instead of eating it; she impulsively popped it into Jeff's mouth. He reached up and snatched her wrist, holding her hand prisoner. After accepting the offered cheese, he gently nibbled her fingertip before sucking it into his mouth. His eyes never left hers.

"You have a finger fetish," she said when he let go.

"I think you pointed that out before." He chuckled. "But I promise, I've only been tempted by yours."

"I feel special," she said with a laugh.

"You are."

Lexi blushed at his comment. They continued to nibble on the food, taking turns feeding each other. When they had their fill, Jeff set the tray on the floor and then rolled over to look at Lexi. They lay side by side, facing each other, resting their heads on pillows while each propping themselves up on an elbow.

Jeff reached out and ran a hand along the side of her hip. He took hold of her dress' skirt and gently inched it upward, revealing first her feminine calf, then her knee, and finally her lower thigh. Lexi silently watched as he tugged on her hem. At one point, she lifted slightly to free the fabric. It slid higher.

Jeff moved his hand from the dress to her bare thigh, lightly massaging the area. Lexi reached out to make her own exploration, running her fingertips over his features, down his neck, and along his bare chest.

When Jeff slipped his hand under the hem of her dress, he discovered she wasn't wearing panties. Smiling, he massaged her bottom and pulled her closer to him. Lexi rolled atop Jeff and the two began to kiss as his hands moved freely over the bare skin of her buttock.

Lexi loved the way he kissed. She loved the way his hard body felt against hers. She loved the way he massaged her bottom. She wanted to remove the dress and feel his nude skin against hers.

"Lexi, wait." Jeff pushed her back slightly, trying to catch his breath. One reason for the intimate setting, he wanted an opportunity to talk to her before… before this. He needed to explain to her about her grandfather so they could move forward without any secrets. If he took extra effort—with the candles and food—she would be more receptive to what he had to say and not push him away.

"I can't wait," Lexi declared in a hoarse whisper. She showed him what she meant when, in the next moment, she reached between them and slipped her hand in the fly of his pajama bottoms. Jeff groaned as the hand wrapped around the already hard shaft.

Unable to think, Jeff forgot about what he needed to say and gave Lexi what she wanted. With a sudden movement, he rolled over, positioning Lexi under him with her legs open and the hem of her dress around her hips. It took minimal effort for Jeff to find his way inside her warmth, guided by the shapely legs wrapped around his waist.

Jeff woke before Lexi on Saturday morning. Sometime during the night, she had removed her dress. His pajama bottoms came off the second time they made love, but he put them on again when he took the food tray to the kitchen.

He still hadn't brought up the subject of her grandfather. Nor did he find the right time after she woke up. He spent Saturday helping her prepare for the Sunday swap meet, promising himself he would tell her later. He just didn't know when later would come.

CHAPTER SIXTEEN

*I*t was still dark when they drove into the parking lot of the London Bridge Shopping Center on Sunday morning. Other vendors were already setting up their booths. Each parking space on the paved lot was numbered, designating merchant spaces. From Monday through Saturday and during the warmer months, the area was a parking lot for the local businesses. On Sundays from September through May, the area became a bustling swap meet. It would be an hour before customers would be arriving, but the area already hummed with activity.

Storefronts, restaurants, and lodge buildings lined the perimeter of the parking lot. To the south beyond the commercial buildings was a view of the London Bridge and to the west a view of Lake Havasu.

Jeff parked next to the space Lexi had rented and

unloaded the vehicle, before moving it outside the vendor area. It was a little chilly, and Lexi was grateful she had returned home that morning and changed into denims and a blouse and had grabbed a jacket. Instead of wearing flip-flops, she wore a pair of socks and jogging shoes. She had spent the last two nights with Jeff.

Before moving the car, Jeff and Lexi erected the EZ-UP and folding table. While Jeff moved the car, Lexi arranged her space, putting up the banners she had made and setting out the pamphlets and business cards she had printed at Staples. From the EZ-UP, she hung mini-posters with photographs of hot fudge sundaes. She had purchased the images online from stock sites, as she hadn't had time to take her own photographs.

Neatly, she placed the glass jars on the table, setting them in rows. Under the table, she stored the ice chest with the fudge samples. By the time Jeff returned, she had finished arranging the table and was already sitting in one of the two folding chairs they'd brought along.

"You're quick," Jeff told her. "It looks good."

"Thanks. I'm excited!" Lexi grinned and then noticed Jeff was carrying a sack.

"What's that?"

"I brought us some coffee and picked up a couple of breakfast burritos when I went to park the car."

"You're awesome."

Jeff sat in the empty chair next to Lexi and handed her a cup of coffee and a burrito. Together, they enjoyed their breakfast while watching the hubbub of activity going on around them. Some vendors had elaborate set-ups and took considerable time arranging their displays. Lexi silently congratulated herself for the relatively easy and quick set-up.

The sun was just starting to rise when the first wave of customers arrived, but none seemed particularly interested in a free hot fudge sample. It wasn't until around 10:30 a.m. that Lexi handed out her first one.

"So how do you put this on ice cream? It's pretty thick. But it's good," one woman said as she spooned out the last of the fudge from the small plastic cup.

"It gets thicker when it cools, but right out of the microwave it's very hot so you need to wait about five minutes before pouring it over your ice cream," Lexi explained. She stood behind the table talking to the woman, as several other silent potential customers tasted their samples. Jeff sat in a chair behind the table, listening.

The lady who asked the question picked up one of the jars and looked at it. "So you make it with this?"

"Yes," Lexi continued. "You add a tablespoon of butter and a tablespoon of drinking water to a cup like this." Lexi held up the 8-ounce Pyrex measuring cup for the people to see. You microwave it for 40 seconds and then stir in two tablespoons of the mix and microwave for 42 seconds."

More people were walking to the table, lured over by the *free hot fudge sample* signs. Jeff got up from the chair and started handing out samples as Lexi answered questions.

"That's it?" the lady asked.

Meanwhile, the other people were commenting on the excellent flavor of the fudge and making jokes about wanting more samples.

"Yes, but it's best to wait at least five minutes before pouring it on your ice cream," Lexi explained.

"But what if I want more than one serving?" someone asked. "Seems like a hassle to make it one at a time."

"You can make more than one serving at a time, but you need to make sure you have a large enough microwave cooking bowl, or it can boil over. You would have to adjust your cooking time," Lexi explained.

"How do I do that?" another asked.

"Here…" Lexi handed the person a brochure she had prepared for such a question.

"While Walt's Hot Fudge on Demand is designed to make single servings of hot fudge, easily in your microwave," Lexi explained to a growing crowd, "I've listed suggested times and sizes of cooking containers for multiple servings. But remember, unlike conventional ovens, microwave ovens don't always cook exactly the same way. So, when you first make the fudge, I suggest starting with the single serving. If you want it to be a little thicker, you might have to cook it a few seconds longer.

"The material of your cooking container—such as a ceramic coffee cup versus a glass measuring cup—and the size of the container—such as an 8-ounce glass measuring cup versus 16-ounce cup—can also effect the cooking times. On this chart, I've listed the recommended cooking times, depending on container size and material."

"Sounds complicated," said the woman asking the original question. Then she asked, "How much does it cost?"

"Twenty dollars for a jar."

In spite of the fact the woman seemed concerned over the inexact nature of cooking times, she handed Lexi a twenty-dollar bill and took a jar. The jars sold quickly, much faster than Lexi had expected, and shortly before noon, all twenty-four jars were gone, as were all the samples.

"I don't believe it!" Lexi exclaimed after she had handed out the last sample and was finally alone with Jeff.

"I think you have a hit."

"It's off to a great start, but it'll really depend on next Sunday, and if I get any feedback from this week's customers. I won't know until then if they liked the mix or not."

"It was a good touch having your Facebook page link on the label and asking them to log in and let you know how they liked the fudge."

"Well, that will depend on if they leave good reviews or bad!"

"Lucky for you, it's possible to delete comments from your Facebook page," Jeff teased.

"Are you all out of samples?" a woman asked. Lexi turned around and faced the man and woman now standing on the other side of the table. The jars were gone, but there were still some brochures and business cards.

"I'm sorry, we're out. But we'll be back next Sunday," Lexi told her. There was something familiar about the couple, but Lexi couldn't figure out what it was. She guessed they were in their mid-fifties, and by the way, they were dressed, it looked as if they were on their way to the golf course.

"I'm sorry to hear that. We overheard some people talking about it on another aisle and we were hoping there was some left." The woman sounded disappointed.

"We'll be back next Sunday."

"Unfortunately, we're leaving for a few weeks. Will you be here in March?"

"I hope so."

"Lexi Beaumont, you sold them all?" Angie seemed to appear out of nowhere, camera in hand.

"Hi, Angie. Yeah, we did."

"That's awesome and all, but I came down to take some photos of your display!"

"We told you to come with us this morning," Jeff teased.

"Yeah, right. I don't think so. It was still dark when you guys left!" Angie laughed.

As the three friends chatted about the successful day, the couple asking for the sample did not leave. Instead, they seemed frozen on the spot, staring at Lexi. They continue to stare until Lexi and her friends noticed.

"Lexi Beaumont, Walt and Susan's daughter?" the woman asking about the fudge blurted out.

Surprised to hear her parents' name she took a closer look at the couple. "Oh my god! Joe and Carolyn Manning!" she cried out.

Carolyn Manning didn't wait for Lexi to come to her. She flew around the table and hugged the young woman. Lexi never imagined she would break into tears at such a reunion, but it was a difficult thing not to do when Carolyn Manning was sobbing and hugging, while her husband stood quietly with tears running down his face.

Angie and Jeff watched silently. Both recognized the couple's names. Finally, Carolyn pulled herself together, as did Lexi. They stood facing each other, each wiping away the tears and smiling.

"I don't know why I didn't recognize you immediately," Carolyn said. "You look just like your mother."

"But she has Walt's green eyes. I swear I see him in her eyes," Joe commented.

"I can't believe this. How long has it been?" Lexi asked excitedly, no longer crying.

"Eleven years," Carolyn said.

"What are you doing in Havasu?" Lexi asked.

"We moved here last year, after Joe retired. There was no way we were going to stay in New York. Neither of us are fond of harsh winters."

"New York? I didn't know you were living there."

Joe and Carolyn exchanged glances.

"Yes, we moved shortly after you went to live with your grandfather. By the way, how is he?"

"I really don't know, but I assume he's fine. I moved out after the first of the year, and you might say we're estranged."

"I'm sorry to hear that, but it doesn't surprise me, considering his relationship with Walt," Joe said.

"Which is one reason I always wondered why he appointed Grandfather as my guardian."

"But Lexi, your parents didn't appoint your grandfather guardian. They appointed us," Carolyn said.

Lexi stood in the London Bridge Shopping Center parking lot, surrounded by vendor booths and noisy shoppers, but no longer heard anything beyond her own thoughts. Transported back in time, she was once again that young girl sitting before the judge, telling him she wanted to live with her grandfather.

"Then it was my fault?" Lexi blurted out.

"What do you mean?" Carolyn asked with a frown.

"Did I go to live with that man because I was a stupid little girl who chose her grandfather? Who asked to live with a man I didn't know? Is that what happened?"

"What are you talking about? You went with your grandfather because he took us to court over your custody. I remember the judge talking to you, but that really had nothing to do with it. Your grandfather is a very powerful man, and we didn't have the resources to fight him. During that same time, Joe was transferred to New York, and we simply did not have the financial resources to stay in California and fight him, and our attorney told us it was a hopeless case."

"But why didn't you stay in touch?" Lexi impulsively blurted, immediately regretting her question.

"Because your grandfather wouldn't allow it. He took out a restraining order against us, and we weren't permitted to contact you. They said it was in your best interests, that you would adjust better if we didn't interfere," Joe explained.

CHAPTER SEVENTEEN

"I remember your father's hot fudge very well," Carolyn reminisced. She and her husband sat with Lexi, Angie, and Jeff in a long booth at the Javelina Cantina Mexican Restaurant, overlooking the London Bridge. At the swap meet, Carolyn had suggested they go somewhere for lunch, since Lexi was out of her hot fudge mix anyway, and it would give them an opportunity to catch up on old times. Joe and Carolyn sat on one side of the booth, while the three younger people sat on the opposite side, with Lexi in the middle.

"Do you recall that weekend we spent at my cousin's cabin in Wrightwood? You were probably eight or nine years old," Carolyn asked. "It was really late and everyone was asleep. Your mom and I got the urge for a hot fudge sundae, but we only had a little ice cream left."

"I remember." Lexi smiled at the memory. She took a tortilla chip from a basket sitting in the middle of the table. "Not sure if the smell of the hot fudge woke me or your giggling." She dipped the chip in a bowl of salsa and took a bite.

"You made us split it with you. Threatened you would wake Joe and your dad if we refused." They all laughed.

"Those were good times." Carolyn sighed.

Everyone was silent for a few moments, lost in private thoughts, when the server arrived with their food. Plates were passed around the table, and drink glasses refilled. Jeff ordered another Corona and handed the server his empty bottle. When the server finally completed his tasks at the table, the conversation resumed.

"I still don't understand," Jeff asked. "Why did the courts give her grandfather custody?"

"Just because parents assign a guardian in a will, that doesn't necessarily mean their wishes will be honored," Joe explained. "Especially when the appointed guardian isn't a family member and a family member contests the will."

"It also helps," Carolyn added, "if the family member is very wealthy and has connections."

"I still say it didn't help when I told the judge I wanted to live with my grandfather. I can't help but wonder how things might have been different had I given another answer."

"I really don't think it would have changed the outcome. Your answer only made the judge feel better about the decision he'd already made." Carolyn reached across the table and patted Lexi's hand. "I'm so sorry, Lexi; I had no idea things had been so awful for you."

"Carolyn, it wasn't that bad," Lexi said brightly, not wanting to make her parents' best friends feel guilty over something they couldn't change. "I lived in a very nice house, and I wasn't abused in any way. I had plenty to eat, clothes to wear, and received a nice education. It was just that he was always gone, and I was pretty much raised by the servants."

"It sounds lonely," Carolyn said sadly.

"Let's not forget the old S.O.B. tried to marry you off to his partner!" Angie added, sounding annoyed.

"He what?" Carolyn gasped. Both she and Joe turned to look at Angie.

"After Lexi graduated, he expected her to marry his business partner. When she refused, he kicked her out and kept everything he ever bought her and everything in her bedroom, which was practically everything she owned, including her clothes."

"Oh, Lexi! I'm so sorry!" Carolyn shook her head in disgust.

"Are you talking about Jerome Peters?" Joe asked.

"Yes," Lexi confirmed.

"He's just a couple of years younger than your dad. What was your grandfather thinking?"

"I really don't know, Joe." Lexi shrugged, grabbing another chip. "Knowing Grandfather, having me marry Peters was the same as marrying off his business and keeping his life all neat and organized. His first priority was always the company. All that doesn't matter to me anymore."

"Lexi surprised her grandfather," Angie chimed in. "He expected her to buckle when he took everything away from her. He didn't realize Lexi freelanced during college and had a nice little nest egg to fall back on."

"What about your inheritance?" Joe asked.

"Inheritance?" Lexi frowned.

"You were supposed to get that when you turned twenty-one. You're twenty-one now, aren't you?"

"I don't know what you mean by inheritance, but there wasn't any from my parents."

"What are you talking about?" Joe asked. "I know your parents had at least $100,000 equity in their house. I remember when he bought it, before you were born, and how much they paid. Housing prices went up like crazy during that decade."

"Not to mention the life insurance money," Carolyn added.

"Life insurance? I don't know anything about that. According to my grandfather, whatever money there was, went to him, to pay off some loan Dad owed him. Apparently, my parents borrowed money from my grandfather."

"What?" Joe and Carolyn shouted at the same time.

"That is utter bullshit!" Joe said, his face turning red.

"Shhh, Joe, not so loud. People are staring." Carolyn patted her husband's arm.

He took a deep breath and lowered his voice. "Lexi, your parents never borrowed money from your grandfather. I would bet my life on that. I don't know what bullshit your grandfather is trying to feed you, but he is lying, plain and simple."

"Lexi, it seems we made a big mistake by walking away and letting your grandfather win. I am so sorry," Carolyn apologized. "At the time... Well, it was all so emotional. Joe had just received his transfer to the New York office, and we weren't in the position to turn it down. At the time, your grandfather presented a good argument to the court. He was your only living relative. He was more than financially equipped to give you whatever you needed. And if you went with us, you'd be leaving your school and friends, and so soon after your parents' death."

"What was this about a court order?" Jeff asked, breaking into the conversation. "Back at the swap meet you said something about a restraining order."

"Soon after Lexi went to live with her grandfather, we moved. I regularly sent letters and gifts to Lexi, yet never heard back. About a year after her parents' death, we came to California for a visit and wanted to spend some time with Lexi. We weren't permitted to see her, and when we pressed the issue, her grandfather got a restraining order. She was a minor, and he was her guardian, so the judge agreed he had the right to deny us visits. I suppose we crossed over the line by showing up at her school, but we didn't know what else to do."

"I never knew you wrote or sent gifts. And I didn't know about your visit to my school."

"We never managed to see you, but apparently, your Grandfather suspected we might do something like that, so he hired someone to follow us while we were in California."

He hired someone to follow us while we were in California—those words made Jeff feel a little sick inside. *I need to tell her*, Jeff told himself. Yet, he hadn't been able to find the right time. He wondered how she would feel when she found out her grandfather had also hired him to follow her.

"You need to find out about your inheritance," Carolyn told Lexi.

"I don't even know where to start."

"I'll help you." Jeff wrapped one arm around Lexi and gave her a reassuring hug, pulling her closer to him in the booth.

"So, tell me, how long have you and Jeff been together?" Carolyn asked.

"I think the more interesting question," Angie teased, "is how long they've known each other."

Lexi elbowed her friend.

"Ouch!" Angie squealed.

"I'm sorry. I didn't mean to pry," Carolyn said.

The next moment the server returned to the table. He refilled their beverage glasses and asked how they were enjoying their food. He offered to bring more chips, to which they declined. When he left again, Joe asked Lexi how she came up with her idea for marketing the hot fudge sauce. The conversation took several turns during the meal. From hot fudge they moved on to Joe's retirement; how they all ended up in Havasu. They were discussing upcoming local events when the server came to remove their plates.

Joe asked the server to bring him the check, and despite some friendly arguments from his dining companions, who each offered to pay, the server took Joe's credit card a few minutes later. After the bill was paid, the five got up from the booth and made their way from the dining room, down the short hallway between the bar and kitchen, to the front entrance of the restaurant.

Joe had parked his vehicle near the stairs by the front entrance, while Angie and Jeff had parked around back, toward the Channel. The five lingered by Joe's car while saying their goodbyes. Lexi and Carolyn exchanged phone numbers, and Carolyn promised she would call Lexi as soon as they returned to Havasu from the trip they were taking.

After the group said their lengthy goodbyes, Joe and Carolyn got into their vehicle, and the three younger people began walking to the rear parking area.

"They seem like really nice people," Jeff commented a few moments later, after Joe drove out of the parking lot with Carolyn.

"Yeah, they were always nice to me when I was a kid."

"I think you need to check into this inheritance thing," Angie suggested.

"I didn't want to say anything back at the restaurant," Lexi said as the three stopped by Angie's Volkswagen. "I'm sure they're wrong about the inheritance."

"Why do you say that? They seemed to know there was life insurance, and they were both adamant your parents wouldn't have borrowed money from your grandfather," Angie argued.

"Even best of friends don't always know what goes on behind closed doors. About two years before my parents were killed, I overheard them arguing. I remember because my parents never fought, and this one was pretty heated. They didn't know I was in the next room, because I was supposed to be outside, but I had come in to get something."

"What did you overhear?" Jeff asked.

"They were arguing about money. My dad had a small business, and I guess things were going bad, and he needed to replace some equipment. My mother suggested he go to his father for a loan, and that is when the fighting started.

"Plus, I don't see how my grandfather could hide something like an inheritance from me. If there was life insurance money, then wouldn't he have to put it in some sort of savings under my name? And if they were having money problems, they probably didn't pay the premiums or cashed out the policy. There are lots of possibilities, and the less likely, in my opinion, is that there is some unclaimed inheritance out there waiting for me."

"Shouldn't you at least check into it?"

"I don't know, Angie. I'd rather focus on positive stuff, and at the moment, one of the most positive things in my life—from a financial perspective—is the hot fudge mix business. And, guys, I sold out today! *Woohoo!*"

CHAPTER EIGHTEEN

Angie drove the red Volkswagen out of the Javelina Cantina parking lot as Lexi and Jeff got into Jeff's vehicle. After closing the car doors, they sat quietly for a moment, looking out the front windshield at the back of the restaurant.

Lexi was playing over the day's events in her mind, and didn't noticed when Jeff turned in her direction and silently studied her profile. When she finally noticed he was watching her, she turned to him and gave him an inquisitive frown.

"What?" she asked.

In response, Jeff reached out and gently brushed the side of her face with the back of his hand. The hand lingered for a moment, moving over her soft cheek in a feather-light back-and-forth caress.

"You're so beautiful," he whispered before withdrawing his hand.

Lexi blushed at the compliment and couldn't decide on an appropriate response, so she said nothing.

"Lexi, does Angie have a problem with you and me?"

"No, why do you ask that?"

"The crack in the restaurant; how we haven't known each other long."

"Oh, that." Lexi smiled. "That's just Angie, she likes to tease. No, she likes you."

"I know things have happened fast."

"It's been kind of crazy."

"Lexi, I only have the rental until the end of the month."

"I remember you mentioned that before. But I didn't think it was a definite thing. The end of the month… that's Thursday."

"I hoped I could work something out."

"Does this mean you're leaving?" The twisting in Lexi's stomach made her want to cry, but she remained outwardly calm.

"No, but I need to start looking for someplace else to stay. I'm not in a hurry to go back home."

"But, you have to go back to work eventually. I imagine your employer expects you to return sometime, and if you find something else before you do, you'll have to move to wherever the job is. I guess I always knew. I just didn't want to think about it."

"You aren't listening to me, Lexi. I'm not planning

to leave Havasu right away. I don't want to leave you."

Leaning toward Jeff, Lexi brushed her lips over his and then pulled away. Jeff captured the side of her face in the palm of his hand and ever so gently moved his thumb over her skin as he looked into her eyes.

"Can we talk about this later? So much has happened today. I don't think I can deal with the thought of you leaving, yet I can't help but feel guilty, knowing what it might mean if you stay."

"You have absolutely nothing to feel guilty about," he told her.

"I don't want to do anything to jeopardize your job or hurt your potential job opportunities. I know you've had a number of interviews, and if you're offered one you want, you need to go."

"Are you trying to get rid of me?"

"Now you aren't listening to me!" Lexi leaned toward Jeff again, resting her head against his shoulder. Wrapping his arms around her, he held her tight and kissed the top of her head.

"Don't worry about me, Lexi. I just wanted you to know I would be looking for another place to stay in Havasu."

"Do you think he wants to stay here?" Angie asked

Lexi that evening when she learned Jeff wouldn't be their neighbor for much longer. Angie sat at the breakfast bar eating a hot fudge sundae while Lexi stood in the kitchen making a peanut butter sandwich.

"Here? No. Why do you ask that?"

"Well, you two… you know." Angie shrugged.

"No. I wouldn't even suggest that. In fact, I wouldn't want that. I like him. I mean, I really like him. I might even be in love with him. But I'm not totally stupid. We've only known each other for a few weeks."

"Good. I like him, too. But I confess; I was a little concerned you two were moving awful fast. And while I suppose all that's cool, moving in together would be pushing it."

"He's been wonderful and supportive. We talk about all sorts of things, but when it comes to his job and how he's able to be here, and what kind of work he's doing by telecommuting, it isn't all that clear to me."

"You don't think he's into something illegal, do you?"

"Illegal? No. That never entered my mind."

"It's just that most guys love to talk about their jobs. At least the guys I've dated."

"Well, I do know he goes online several hours a day. Not sure if it's work related or job hunting." Lexi took a bite of her peanut butter sandwich.

"Then I would stop stressing about it, Lexi. The guy is obviously crazy about you. Considering the number of people who work from home on the computer, I'm sure his current employer is okay with him being here. And if he is offered a job he really wants, I'm sure he'll do what's necessary for his career."

Lexi's cellphone let out a little beep, indicating an incoming text message. She picked it up from the kitchen counter. Continuing to eat her sandwich, she read the message.

"It's Jeff. He wants me to come over and sit in the spa with him." Lexi smiled. She held the sandwich in her mouth as she used her fingers to send a reply message.

"Should I expect you home tonight?" Angie asked, already knowing the answer.

"Nope," Lexi chirped cheerfully.

Angie watched Lexi leave. To the empty, room she said, "I think we are in denial, Lexi. Looks like you two are already living together."

THE NEXT MORNING, LEXI TURNED ON HER COMPUTER and logged into her Facebook account. Wearing her robe, she sat on the loveseat in Jeff's living room with the laptop on her knees. Jeff was just handing her a cup of coffee when she let out a little whooping sound.

"I don't believe it!"

Jeff stood silently beside her, a warm coffee mug in his hand, waiting for her to explain.

"Six of those people who bought my hot fudge mix have already posted on my Facebook page. They are all giving rave reviews!"

"That's great! I told you you had a hit."

"Not just that, but they are sharing with friends. Already people are responding. Jeff, I only sold 24 jars, but the page has 112 likes! How is that possible?"

"The power of social media." Jeff sat next to her on the small couch and looked over at her laptop screen.

"I want to prepare forty-eight jars this week— four cases."

"You might as well. Even if you don't sell them, they'll keep for the next Sunday."

"Wow, someone asked where they can order the mix online!"

"Ahh, my little hot fudge mogul." Jeff wrapped his arm around her shoulders and gave her a kiss on the cheek.

"This is so exciting."

"Yes, but one step at a time. I think selling it online is inevitable, but this thing is moving pretty quickly, considering you came up with the idea just a few weeks ago. How about we sit down this after-noon and review your business plan again. If you don't get organized early on, you'll regret it later, especially if this thing really takes off."

Sugar Rush. The term flashed through Lexi's mind. Isn't that what Jeff said when he had first approached her in the grocery store? Smiling to herself, she couldn't help but think that was a sweet metaphor for her relationship with Jeff and the hot fudge venture.

THAT AFTERNOON ANGIE JOINED LEXI AND JEFF IN THE spa, where the three discussed the hot fudge business at length while drinking cold beer. For dinner, Jeff barbecued chicken at his house for the three of them. Later that evening, Angie walked back to her house, and Lexi stayed with Jeff.

The week moved quickly toward the weekend, and Lexi kept busy. On Tuesday morning, Jeff took her shopping so she could purchase more jars, mix ingredients, and food products she wanted to high-light in promotional photos for the hot fudge sauce. When she got home from the store, she put the jars through the dishwasher and then added the mix after the jars dried.

On Wednesday, Lexi cooked up a batch of fudge on the stove. Angie helped with a photo shoot, taking digital pictures of the hot fudge sauce used in various ways. They made a traditional sundae, topped a brownie sundae and poured the sauce over bananas and strawberries. Jeff was there to eat up the sweet props when they finished with each shoot.

The three continued to have dinners together. On Tuesday, they had Italian food at Mario's Italian Restaurant, and on Wednesday, Angie insisted on Italian food again, this time taking the threesome to Angelina's Italian Kitchen. Over dessert, they debated over which was the best Italian restaurant of the two, and finally decided it was a draw. They enjoyed them both.

When it came time to go to bed, Lexi always stayed with Jeff, and Angie wondered what her friend would do when Jeff moved to another location. From what Angie understood, Jeff was waiting to hear back from a Realtor regarding available rentals. With the number of winter visitors in town, rentals were scarce. When Angie asked Jeff if other renters were moving into his house on the first, Jeff said he didn't think so. Angie then asked why he didn't simply keep that house. In a cryptic fashion, he said it was complicated, but he was looking into it.

Lexi spent most of Thursday on the computer, updating her social media sites. She scheduled Twitter tweets, uploaded photos to the Facebook page, and created a board at Pinterest, where she added dessert pictures.

Jeff rescued her late Thursday afternoon and insisted he take her to dinner.

"Where's Angie?" Jeff asked shortly after he arrived.

"Don't you remember? She had a job this afternoon."

"Oh, that's right. Some real estate thing?"

"Yep. A Realtor hired her to take pictures at an open house. I don't expect her back for a couple of hours."

"So, let's go get something to eat."

"Jeff, we went out the last two nights."

"I'm not suggesting Italian."

Lexi laughed. "Yeah, I don't think I could do another night of Italian, but I have to admit Havasu has two damn good Italian restaurants."

"I understand they have a good steakhouse, too. I asked the guy at the gas station where I could get a good steak. He said Rod's Homestead. It's sort of a rustic, cowboy-looking place. Come on. You need to get away from that damn computer."

"What's going on with the rental? The other day you said you needed to get out by the end of the month. It's the end of the month."

"Well, I haven't heard back from the landlord, so I assume I can stay a few extra days. Like I said, it's complicated."

Since Beaumont had threatened to fire Jeff if Lexi didn't return home within a week, Jeff had talked to him one more time. That phone call was brief, and instead of issuing additional threats, Beaumont simply asked for an update and then hung up. Jeff contacted the Realtor who'd rented the house to Beaumont, telling him he would like to pay for February, but because the rental was currently in Beaumont's name, the Realtor told Jeff he would get back to him. Jeff still had not heard back from the Realtor.

Tonight, after dinner, I will sit Lexi down and tell her everything, Jeff told himself. It was something he said every night that week.

CHAPTER NINETEEN

"Oh my gawd, I'm so stuffed," Lexi groaned as she leaned back in the leather car seat. Jeff chuckled, but continued to look ahead as he steered the car down the highway, heading home.

"I can't believe you ate that entire porterhouse."

"It was delicious. But it was big, wasn't it?" Lexi moaned.

"So, you won't be having a hot fudge sundae with me when we get home?"

"Please, you're going to make me throw up!"

"Does this mean you won't order the porterhouse the next time we go to Rods?"

"Hell no," Lexi snapped. "It just means I'll eat less of the baked potato."

"Are you sure about that?" he teased.

"Well, maybe I won't eat the salad. That smoky baked potato was pretty good, too. Thanks for taking me to dinner, Jeff. But really, you need to start letting me pay."

They were quiet for a few moments when Lexi asked, "Any luck at finding a new job, or are you just going to stay where you are?"

"I was considering applying with this little start up business I came across."

"Really? Doing what?"

"Production management. I think I could be a valuable asset for the company."

"Great, where's it located?" Lexi tried to sound upbeat, but she held her breath wondering where this new job might take him.

"Currently Lake Havasu City, Arizona, but I don't think the owner of the company is committed to the location." It took Lexi a few seconds to register what he was saying, and once she did, she wasn't certain if he was sincere or joking around.

"Are you serious?"

"Very. It's not going to be long before you outgrow your swap meet operation. If this thing takes off, it won't be practical packaging and shipping the product out of your kitchen. You are excellent at marketing, and I believe I can develop an efficient plan to package and ship the product."

Jeff had just turned the corner onto their street, about ready to pull into his driveway when he noticed lights on in his house.

"That's strange. I don't remember leaving the

lights on." After pulling into the driveway, he turned off the engine.

"It wasn't dark when we left, you just didn't notice. Now, come on. Let's go inside. I want to interview you."

Both laughing, they each got from the vehicle and shut their car doors, walking together to the front entry. Lexi again asked Jeff if he was serious. She watched him unlock the front door. Jeff entered the house first, paying more attention to what Lexi was asking than what might be waiting for him in the house.

Lexi followed Jeff inside. He kept his eyes on her while they talked, not paying attention to where he was walking. When Lexi froze in her steps and stared blankly ahead, he stopped talking and turned to see what had captured her attention.

"Grandfather," Lexi said at last.

Ethan Beaumont sat on the living room recliner, observing the new arrivals with keen interest. With his elbows propped on the chair's arms, he held his hands together as he absently tapped his knuckles against his chin. Overdressed for Havasu, he wore a gray business suit.

"What are you doing in Jeff's house?"

"Hello, Granddaughter. I see you've been a busy girl since you ran away from home."

"Ran away? From what I remember, I was kicked out. But you haven't answered my question. What are you doing in Jeff's house?" The blood in her veins raced and her heart pounded. If she didn't know better, she would swear the top of her head was about to explode.

"Jeff's house? Actually, it's my house, considering I'm the one who's been paying the rent." Beaumont shifted his gaze from Lexi to Jeff. "Barnett, I'm very disappointed in you. Imagine my displeasure at having to hire someone to spy on the person I hired to spy on Lexi. I was not paying you to seduce my granddaughter."

"What are you talking about?" Lexi asked.

"Ask J.B. here. He's been watching you since you left my house. Amazingly, he was able to rent the apartment right across the hall from yours."

Lexi turned to look at Jeff, waiting for him to deny the accusation.

"I can explain," Jeff began.

"I'm sure you can," Ethan interrupted. "Tell me again, J.B., because I can't remember. Did you ever install that surveillance equipment at the apartment, or did you wait and install it at their house here?"

"Surveillance equipment!" Lexi shrieked.

"No, Lexi, I never did that," Jeff said, panicky and uncertain how to explain while Beaumont sat there, calmly taunting him.

"It's simple Lexi," Ethan interrupted, "Jeff Barnett has been in my employ for two years now. You've heard me talk about J.B."

Lexi looked from her grandfather to Jeff. While she had never met Ethan Beaumont's personal assistant, her grandfather occasionally mentioned him, always referring to the employee as J.B. She felt as if someone had just smashed an iron skillet across the back of her head when she remembered the bearded neighbor. Now she knew why she and Angie thought there was something familiar about Jeff. He was the creepy neighbor who was always listening to them.

"You!" Lexi gasped, suddenly feeling sick. She took a step back away from Jeff.

"Lexi, let's leave and let me explain," Jeff said in a panic.

"I certainly hope you don't intend to leave in my car," Beaumont interjected. "I've come to pick up the car and take Lexi home."

Wild eyed, Lexi looked from Jeff to her grandfather. "I'm not going anywhere with you!" Lexi shouted. "And you," she went on, now looking at Jeff, her voice shaky, "I never want to see you again!"

Lexi turned abruptly and ran from the house. Pausing just a moment, Jeff ran after her. In his haste, he tripped when going down the front steps, sending him sprawling on the ground. By the time he got back on his feet and started toward Lexi, she was almost at her house. By the time he reached her driveway, she had gone inside and slammed the door shut.

"Lexi, please. We have to talk!" Jeff shouted a few moments later as he stood on her porch and pounded on her front door.

"This is Angie," said a stern voice from inside the house. "Lexi is very upset. I want you to leave now. If you keep pounding on the door, I'll call the police. Do you understand?"

Broken, Jeff turned away and headed back to his house. He found Beaumont still sitting on the recliner.

"I failed to mention it earlier, but you're fired," Beaumont said dispassionately, when Jeff entered the house.

"You can't fire me, I quit."

"Good. I accept your resignation. Makes it more difficult for you to collect unemployment." With measured calm, Beaumont stood and faced Jeff. The younger man struggled to maintain his composure.

"I'll be back in the morning to make sure you've moved out. Leave my car in the garage. Don't try to rent the house for February; I've already paid for the month."

Beaumont arrogantly walked past Jeff, obviously not concerned the young man might get physical. Their shoulders brushed, and Beaumont nudged Jeff aside. Standing in the doorway, preparing to exit, he turned around one last time and faced Jeff.

"Stay away from my granddaughter. You totally fucked this thing up. I don't know what the hell you thought you were doing encouraging her in this harebrained fudge business. If you think you can get your hands on my company by screwing my granddaughter, you're even stupider than Lexi."

Had Lexi's grandfather not been in his eighties, Jeff would have planted his fist in the man's arrogant face. He didn't care what Beaumont said about him, but the way he talked about Lexi infuriated him. He silently watched as the elderly man made his way down the walkway. It was then Jeff noticed Ethan's car parked across the street. He hadn't noticed it when he had come home from dinner.

Five minutes later, he frantically paced the floor, the cellphone in his hand. He tried calling Lexi, but her answer machine picked up. When he sent her a text message, he received a response, but not from her. *This is Angie. I've been instructed to delete your text messages. She doesn't want to read them and neither do I. Delete.*

Sickened, Jeff considered his options. A few minutes later, he sat down at his computer and wrote Lexi a letter. After printing it out, he began to pack his things. He doubted he would be able to get a rental car this late in the evening, so he looked through the phone book, searching for a taxi or shuttle service to take him to a hotel. He stacked his suitcases by the front door, then went to the walk-in-closet and stared at the boxes neatly stacked along the wall.

He already knew what he was going to do. It came to him when he was writing the letter. He couldn't take the boxes with him; they belonged to Lexi. He couldn't leave them in the house, because her grandfather would throw them away and then the old son of a bitch would go home and fire his housekeeper.

One by one, Jeff carried the boxes to Lexi and Angie's and set them by the front door. It took him twenty minutes before he finished delivering all the boxes, stacking them in neat piles. On the drive to Lake Havasu City, the boxes had filled the back seat and trunk of the car, yet now it didn't seem like there were that many, not when one considered they supposedly held everything Lexi owned when she left the estate. He wondered what that said about her life with her wealthy grandfather.

After leaving the boxes, he brought over the items Lexi had left in his garage, including the EZ-UP, folding table, ice chest, and camp chairs.

Jeff knocked on the door and waited.

"I told you I would call the police. I mean it," came Angie's terse voice.

"I understand, but I brought over Lexi's things, and they're here by the front door. I don't want to just leave them. Someone might take them before morning."

Assuming he was talking about the items Lexi used at the swap meet, Angie told him to leave and promised she would bring in the things after he was gone. Jeff tucked the letter he had written to Lexi in one of the boxes, then turned and headed back to his house. The boxes were still sitting outside when the shuttle service arrived to take him to the hotel.

CHAPTER TWENTY

ngie peeked out the front window. She had turned off the outside light forty minutes earlier and couldn't see what Jeff had left on the porch. Lexi was in her bedroom, still sobbing inconsolably. Angie thought it was probably a good thing she didn't own a firearm or she might have blown Jeff's head off when he came pounding on the front door. He was gone now, and she figured it was probably safe going outside to bring in Lexi's things. It wasn't just Jeff she wanted to avoid; there was Ethan Beaumont to consider. Angie didn't know if Lexi's grandfather was at Jeff's house. Perhaps he was outside, waiting to bully his way into the house.

Still peeking out the window, she flipped on the outside light, illuminating the front porch. To her surprise, a number of boxes were stacked on the pavers. She knew Lexi didn't have that much stuff over at Jeff's house. Cautiously, she unlocked the front door and opened it slightly, sticking her head outside.

The moon illuminated the street and yard, and there didn't seem to be anyone lurking in the shadows. Stepping on the porch, she walked to the stack of boxes and removed a lid from one. Frowning, she looked inside. It contained Lexi's clothes; she recognized them. They weren't clothes her friend had purchased at the thrift store. They were what Lexi had worn when she was still in college. Hastily, Angie removed some of the other lids and saw the boxes contained Lexi's belongings; things Ethan Beaumont had confiscated when Lexi refused to marry Jerome Peters.

Looking around nervously, Angie placed the lids back on the boxes and then began bringing them into the house. She moved quickly, jittery that Jeff or Ethan might suddenly appear.

After bringing in the boxes, she dragged in the EZ-UP, and then the folding table, ice chest, and camp chairs. Before coming into the house, Angie ran to the end of the driveway and looked down the street, to the house Jeff had been renting. The lights were all out, and there was no car in the driveway. It looked as if no one was home. Running back to her house, Angie closed the door behind her and locked it.

"Lexi?" Angie called out softly a few minutes

later. She stood outside her friend's bedroom, tapping her knuckles against the paneled door. There was no sound coming from the room. Lexi either had stopped crying, or had fallen asleep. Angie stopped knocking. She wondered if she should wait until the morning to tell Lexi about the boxes and let her sleep. In the next moment, the door opened.

"Yeah?" Lexi said wearily. Disheveled, Lexi looked at Angie through red-rimmed eyes. Her hair desperately needed combing, but neither girl cared.

"You need to come see what is in the living room."

"It isn't Jeff or my grandfather?" Lexi stepped backwards, into the bedroom.

"No." Angie reached out and took one of Lexi's hands. "It isn't a person. Come, you need to see this."

Lexi let Angie lead her out into the living room, where a stack of boxes awaited. "What's this?" she asked with a frown.

Angie let go of Lexi's hand and walked around to the other side of the boxes, still facing her friend. "I think it's all your stuff you left at your grandfather's house."

"I don't understand." Lexi walked to the boxes and started removing the lids. "I still don't understand; where did all this stuff come from?"

"Jeff brought them over. Do you think your grandfather brought them to Havasu?"

Lexi was considering that possibility, but then she

froze and started shaking her head. "No, Jeff's had them all along."

"How do you know?"

"I saw these boxes stacked in the master closet in Jeff's bedroom."

"What did he say they were?"

"I never asked. They were shoved to the back of the closet, and I just assumed they belonged to the owner of the house."

Lexi sat on the floor and started going through the boxes, one by one.

"Wow. I never thought I'd see any of this again. I wonder why Grandfather gave these to Jeff."

"You think he did?"

"I don't see how else Jeff got my things."

"Would you like some green tea?"

"Sure. That sounds great."

Angie went to make some tea while Lexi sorted through the boxes. It didn't take long to go through the first three; they contained clothes. The fourth box held some of her mementos that she had stored in her closet back at her grandfather's house. She wondered who had transferred her things from the boxes in her closet into these new ones. Shoes filled the fifth box. On top of the shoes was a folded piece of paper.

Her first impulse was to toss the paper aside, believing it was trash, but then she paused and unfolded it. It was a typed letter. Her eyes flashed to the bottom of the page; it was from Jeff. A half an hour earlier, she would have torn it up and refused to read it. Since she had stopped crying, she had started asking questions. Alone in her bedroom, there was no one to give her answers. Perhaps this letter would tell her what she needed to know.

Dear Lexi, I am not asking you to forgive me, but I think you have the right to know what all of this is about. I hope you don't tear up the letter before reading it, because I feel you need to know some things about your grandfather and about me.

Most of what I told you about me was not a lie. I'm from Portland. I have my master's in business, and I did start working with my current employer right after college. What I didn't tell you was that the company I work for belongs to your grandfather. Actually, he is no longer my current employer. Your grandfather fired me tonight, right before I was about to quit.

When he kicked you out of the house, he gave me an unusual assignment. I was to keep an eye on you. His story at the time was that you were vulnerable, and he did not want someone taking advantage of you. I tried to tell him that was not within my job description—but I imagine you know how that went.

I suspect there are several reasons he picked me. One, I was his personal assistant and had signed a confidentiality agreement, so he knew he could trust me to keep quiet. The second reason, when I was in college I worked for an elec-

tronic store, and I know my way around surveillance equipment.

I was instructed to install surveillance equipment in your apartment to keep closer tabs on you. I confess I purchased the equipment, but I never installed it. When it came time to do so, I couldn't. I didn't know you and Angie at the time, but it felt too much like an invasion of your privacy, so I stalled your grandfather.

I rented the apartment across the hall from you. I then realized I could no longer work for your grandfather under these conditions, so I started looking for another job. By the time you decided to go to Havasu, I knew your grandfather would send someone else if I refused to go and just quit.

I need you to know; I never told your grandfather about your hot fudge venture. I was serious when I said I thought it was a great idea.

I think I know why your grandfather wants you to marry Jerome Peters. Peters is the only person he trusts to take over his business. Since they are partners, Peters will continue to own a large share of the company when your grandfather dies. I believe the thought of the company being torn apart at that time, divided between the interests of his heirs and Peters', troubles your grandfather. The only way he can feel secure that won't happen is if Peter's children are his great-grandchildren. To do that, Peters must marry you.

Your grandfather's behavior in all of this has not been rational, and I have to wonder if he is suffering from some age-related dementia. In his efforts to manipulate you, he even went so far as to instruct me to get hold of your checkbook, so he could find a way to drain your bank account. My response to him was that you had little money.

My biggest regret is not coming to you sooner with what was going on. Ironically, I intended to tell you every-thing after dinner tonight, but then your grandfather showed up.

After I finish this letter, I will bring over the boxes. If you are reading this, then you obviously have them. Your grandfather instructed the housekeeper to pack up your belongings and throw them out. She couldn't bring herself to do that, but did not want to lose her job. I offered to take the boxes and keep her secret. So please, no matter how much you hate me now, please don't let your grandfather know you have them. If you do, she will undoubtedly lose her job.

I am sorry I hurt you. I never wanted to do that. I think I first fell in love with you when I saw your portrait at your grandfather's office. Maybe that is why I didn't put up much of an argument when first given the assignment. It gave me the opportunity to get close to you.

Please hold onto your dream. Don't let your grandfa-ther's actions and my part in all this paralyze you.

You have one secret weapon against the manipulations of your grandfather—and that is that he doesn't know you. He really has no idea how bright, special, and creative you are.

I'm leaving the house and staying at a hotel tonight. I'll have to rent a car to go back to California, because the one I was using belongs to the company. You need to know your grandfather has rented the Havasu house for February. I don't know if he intends to use it, or install someone in it to watch you.

If you need to contact me, you have my cell number. Please know, I am on your side, Lexi. I've always been.

With love, Jeff

LEXI SAT FROZEN, HOLDING THE LETTER IN HER HANDS, staring at the words. She didn't quite know what to think. Silent tears slid down her face.

Angie walked into the living room carrying two cups of hot tea. "Here's your tea." She set Lexi's cup on the glass coffee table. Lexi quickly wiped away the tears, using the back of her hand.

"What are you reading?" Angie asked as she sat on the recliner.

"It's a letter from Jeff. It was in one of the boxes."

"Well, that was pretty sneaky of him, the jerk."

"Angie, I want you to read it and tell me what you think."

"Okay." Angie set her tea on the side table and reached over, taking the sheet of paper from Lexi. Settling back in the chair, she read the letter while Lexi silently watched.

"Wow," Angie whispered when she finished. "He doesn't sound like such a jerk."

"I don't know what to think. I'm still numb."

"What do you want to do about your grandfather? Do you want to leave Havasu?"

"No! Absolutely not. I refuse to spend the rest of my life running away from him. Eventually, he'll get the message I won't be forced into an arranged marriage. If he starts bothering me, I'll go down to the police department and see about getting a restraining order."

"You think you can get one?"

"I don't know, but I'm willing to try."

"Are you going to call Jeff?"

"I don't think so. I feel a little better about him. I suppose he was just another person my grandfather manipulated. I can understand he was trying to keep his job until he found something else. But the lies. If he had just been upfront with me, told me what my grandfather was up to… Instead, he chose to lie to me. I really can't get beyond that."

"I understand," Angie said sadly. "It's just that I really did like the guy."

"Yeah, me, too."

Neither one mentioned the fact that Jeff had professed his love in the letter. Yet, they both thought about it.

CHAPTER TWENTY-ONE

Together, Angie and Lexi moved the boxes into the spare bedroom. Glad to have her wardrobe and other personal items back, Lexi shoved the outfits—now wrinkled—back into their respective boxes until laundry day.

"Do you want to talk?" Angie asked when they were finished.

"Not now. I just want to go to bed. I'm exhausted."

Angie gave her friend a hug and told her to sleep well.

THE NEXT MORNING, PERSISTENT KNOCKING AT THE front door woke Angie. Cursing under her breath, she stumbled out of bed and pulled on her robe. The knocking continued. She walked to the living room and glanced down the hallway leading to Lexi's room. Her friend was either sleeping or ignoring the noise.

She looked through the front door's peephole. It was Ethan Beaumont and another man she didn't know. If she hadn't recognized Lexi's grandfather, she would have guessed they were Jehovah's Witnesses, since both men wore business suits, and people rarely wore such formal attire in Havasu. Instead of answering the door, Angie opened the front living room window overlooking the porch.

"What do you want?" Angie asked the men. The two seemed surprise when she called out. Apparently, neither one had noticed her opening the window.

"Would you please just open the door? I don't want to talk through the window," Ethan snapped.

"No. You just woke me up, and Lexi is sleeping. What do you want?"

"It's almost ten in the morning. Get my granddaughter up. I want to see her now."

"No, Mr. Beaumont. You upset Lexi last night, and I certainly don't appreciate you having my apartment bugged."

"I never bugged your apartment, young lady. Now please, I want to see my granddaughter. Now," Ethan ordered. He was clearly losing patience. The second man stood stoically, revealing no emotion.

Angie shut the window and locked it. Instead of opening the front door, she went to Lexi's room.

"What's all that noise?" Lexi asked groggily when Angie walked into her room.

"It's your grandfather; he's pounding on the front door. He has some man with him."

"Oh, shit. I don't want to see him. What did he say?"

"For starters, we shouldn't sleep so late."

"Oh, that's so my grandfather. He believes everyone should be up by six."

Lexi sat up in her bed, holding the top of the comforter so it covered her bare breast. Angie grabbed the robe at the foot of the bed and tossed it to Lexi, who quickly put it on.

"So, what does this other man look like?"

"Short, reddish hair, older dude. Kinda pudgy."

"Not a clue. Wondered for a moment if he brought Jerome Peters."

"I know what Peters looks like. It isn't him. So, do you want to talk to him?"

"Not really, I have nothing to say."

"Okay, I'll tell him you don't want to see him."

Angie returned to the living room and opened the window.

"She says she doesn't want to see you," Angie told him.

"Then you can just tell my granddaughter I intend to wait here. I didn't come all this way to play games. I need to be back in California by Monday, and I expect her to come home with me."

"Why do you think she'll do that?"

"It really is none of your business. This is a family affair. Tell her I'm getting impatient."

Ethan said something under his breath to the other man and then went and sat down on one of the patio chairs on the front porch. The other man nodded, then followed Ethan's lead and sat in the second chair.

Angie shut the window and locked it. She returned to Lexi's bedroom.

"He isn't leaving. He's just sitting there on the porch. Want me to call the police?"

"No. I have a better idea. Did you park your car in the garage?"

"No. I parked it on the other side of the garage. Why?"

"Good. That will be better. If we had to open the garage door, he might hear us when we started the car, and get there before we opened the door."

"What are you talking about?"

"Let's get dressed and sneak out the side door of the garage. If you can start the car and get it out of the driveway before he knows what's going on, we can get outa here."

"Leave Havasu?"

"No. I said I don't want to leave Havasu. But just leave for the day. Let him sit here all day, for all I care. I don't want to talk to him, and I resent the fact he assumes he can just demand I let him in our house."

"Fine with me."

Fifteen minutes later, Angie peeked out the front window. The two men remained seated in the patio chairs, talking to each other. She couldn't hear what they were saying, but they didn't seem to be aware of the fact Lexi might slip away.

Off the kitchen was a small hallway leading to the laundry room and garage. Before leaving the house, Angie set the alarm. The two girls slipped quietly into the garage and then out the side door. Hastily, they got into the Volkswagen, and Angie started the engine. Not waiting for it to warm up, she put the car in reverse and backed out the driveway at an acceler-ated speed.

Just as Angie backed onto the street and turned the vehicle, Lexi glanced up at the front porch and saw her grandfather stand up abruptly, obviously surprised at the sudden appearance of the Volkswa-gen. Without looking back, Angie put the car in drive and sped down the street, away from Ethan Beaumont. Both girls started to laugh.

"Damn, that felt good!" Lexi said. "I'm glad you set the alarm. I wouldn't put it past my grandfather to try and get in the house. I'd like to see him explain things to the police if he tried to break in and set off the alarm."

"Where do you want to go?"

"Let's leave the car at the Safeway parking lot. From there we can walk to Rotary beach and pick up the bug later."

"How about breakfast at Makai's?" Angie suggested.

"Sure. That's not far."

Lexi and Angie spent Friday avoiding Ethan Beaumont. Lexi knew she couldn't hide from him forever, but felt some sense of victory avoiding the confrontation for as long as possible. After breakfast, they walked along the boardwalk leading from the English Village to Rotary Park.

"Have you reconsidered whether you are going to call Jeff?"

"When I first heard what he did, I felt so betrayed. After reading his letter and thinking about it all last night, I can understand how he got tangled up in all this. But I don't know if I can get beyond the lies."

"Well, he's out of a job now. What do you think he'll do?"

"I don't know. Maybe he'll move back to Portland to be near his family while he looks for something."

"Why do you think your grandfather is here?"

"To take me home. I can't think of any other reason. One thing about my grandfather—when he gets something in his head, he becomes obsessed."

"I imagine it was difficult for Jeff, being put in that position or risk losing his job."

"Angie, I thought you wanted to kick his ass last night?"

"Well, I did. Now I just sort of feel sorry for him."

"I don't want to think about all that now. I just want my grandfather to go home and leave me alone so I can focus on my hot fudge business and lead my own life."

When Angie and Lexi finally returned to the house late that afternoon, they spied Ethan's car sitting in the front driveway of Jeff's rental.

"It looks like your grandfather is staying at the house. I wonder how long he's planning to stick around," Angie asked as they drove by. Pulling into their driveway, Angie used the automatic garage door opener to open the garage door. She pulled the car inside and closed the door behind them.

"Didn't he tell you he needed to be back by Monday?"

"Yeah."

"I hope he meant that."

Ethan Beaumont didn't try to contact Lexi again on Friday, but they were certain he was staying in the house two doors down, because his car was in the driveway. Lexi woke up on Saturday morning to the sound of her grandfather knocking on the front door.

"This is ridiculous," she muttered as she pulled herself from the bed. Throwing on her robe, she went to the living room. Glancing out the front window, she noticed her grandfather's car parked in their driveway, blocking the garage. She assumed Angie was still sleeping. Combing her fingers through her hair, she took a deep breath before opening the front door.

"No longer hiding?" Ethan smirked, sounding somewhat surprised that Lexi was at the door instead of her friend.

"What do you want?" she asked, ignoring his remark.

"We need to talk. This has gone on long enough." He started to walk in the house, but Lexi blocked his way, refusing to move out of the doorway.

"I didn't invite you in."

"Stop acting like a child."

"I'm not a child. I'm a twenty-one year old woman, and I don't appreciate how you're trying to manipulate my life."

"I don't appreciate your lack of appreciation. After everything I've done for you, this is how you behave?"

Lexi stepped outside and closed the door behind her. Standing on the front porch, her arms wrapped protectively around her robe-clad body, she glanced at the car in the driveway. The man Angie had described was sitting in the driver's seat.

"Who's that?" Lexi nodded toward the car.

"My new personal assistant. Do you intend to discuss this on the front porch?"

"If you have something to say, you can say it here. You're not welcome in my house."

"It's not your house. You're freeloading off your friend. But then, that's what you do."

"What is that supposed to mean?" Lexi snapped.

"When your parents were killed, I took you in and gave you a home. I paid for your education. But instead of living up to your family obligations, you ran off like a spoiled child."

"You didn't have to take me in."

"You would have preferred to be raised in foster care? But since you don't seem to be making an effort to use that education I paid for, I suppose not having the opportunity to go to college would not have been an issue for you. Perhaps I should have let you been raised by the state."

"Or you could have let Joe and Carolyn Manning take me, like my parents wanted."

"I don't know what you're talking about."

"I know my parents wanted them to raise me, and they were willing. But you went to court and fought for custody."

"So, now you're faulting me for wanting to take in my own granddaughter? Are you saying I should have let strangers raise you?"

"You were a stranger to me. You still are. I appreciate the education you gave me. Honestly, I do. But

I'll never marry Jerome Peters. So stop all this. I'm not coming back to California with you. Maybe someday we can have a relationship, but at the moment, I'm still angry over the spying and lies."

Lexi turned to the door and started to open it, but paused and faced her grandfather again. "Please go, and leave me alone. Or I will file a restraining order against you, just like you did to the Mannings. I promise."

Without another word, she went into the house and closed the door.

Jeff stayed two nights at the hotel, hoping Lexi would read his letter and call. When that didn't happen, he began to wonder if she found it. Instead of trying to contact Lexi, he sent a text message to Angie.

Did Lexi find the letter I left in the box? If so did she read it?

Angie responded immediately, texting back with a two-word message: *yes, yes.*

Sickened with bitter regret, Jeff called the rental company and arranged for a car. So preoccupied with recounting all the mistakes he had made in regards to Lexi, he barely noticed the exorbitant price of the rental vehicle, since he would only be taking it one-way.

It was almost 9 p.m. Saturday night, when Jeff pulled into the driveway of his apartment complex. He parked the rented car in guest parking, as his own vehicle occupied his designated space. After turning off the engine, he sat for a few moments in the semi-darkness, his hands gripping the steering wheel.

He no longer had a job. He no longer had Lexi. Losing his job was inevitable, but losing Lexi wasn't. For the thousandth time, he cursed himself for not telling her the truth before her grandfather showed up. Of course, there was no guarantee she wouldn't have still kicked him out, he reminded himself.

Emotionally exhausted, he got out of the vehicle, removed his suitcases from the trunk, and headed toward his apartment. On his way there, he stopped at the mailboxes at the side of the building. Setting his suitcases on the sidewalk, he unzipped the side pocket to the smaller bag and retrieved the key ring he had put there before leaving for Havasu. Keys to his apartment, mailbox, and vehicle were on the ring.

He unlocked his mailbox. Envelopes and magazines overstuffed the box. Still holding the key ring, he tucked the mail under his left arm, grabbed the handles of the suitcases, and started toward his apartment.

Dropping the bags by his front door, he fumbled with the key ring until he found the key he was looking for. After unlocking and opening the door, he reached in, turned on the light, and picked up his bags. He was home.

———

Lexi couldn't help but feel a little guilty dragging Angie from bed so early on a Sunday morning. To Angie's credit, she didn't once moan over the fact it was still dark outside. They'd packed the Volkswagen the night before, barely fitting everything they needed into the small vehicle. As they drove away, they noticed Ethan Beaumont's car still parked at the house where Jeff had stayed.

Although grateful to have Angie's help, Lexi still missed Jeff. They'd had so much fun the previous Sunday. *Had it all been a lie?* she asked herself.

The two young women managed to assemble the EZ-UP in a relatively short time, and Lexi found the overall set up easier than the previous week, since she now knew how she wanted to arrange everything. When they were finished, Angie moved the car to the parking area. When she returned, she didn't bring coffee or breakfast burritos, as Jeff had done the previous week.

A food concession was located five spaces down, and when it opened for business, Angie went to get them coffee and something to eat. By the time she returned, Lexi already had customers gathering around.

"I had this at my sister's house Friday night. I have to get some; my husband loved it," one woman said as she picked up a mason jar from the table. A man tasted a fudge sample, while a couple waited their turn to ask a question. It wasn't even eight in the morning, and already Lexi had sold ten jars. She couldn't believe so many people were trying fudge so early in the morning, considering the slower start the previous week.

The day went quickly, and when Lexi sold her last jar, she couldn't decide which was more unbelievable —that it was already noon or that she had sold all 48 jars by that time.

"Angie, do you know how much we made today?" She was barely able to contain her excitement. They were alone at the booth for the first time since Angie had gone to get breakfast.

"You mean how much *you* made. I'm just here to help. This is your business."

"Seven hundred and twenty dollars!" Lexi squealed. "Of course, that doesn't take into account the cost of the samples, but that wasn't much."

"Wow." Angie was impressed. "You buy dinner."

"Gladly!" Lexi hugged her friend. Angie laughed and hugged her back.

"Did you hear what that lady in the green hat said to me?" Lexi asked.

"I don't recall the lady; so many people were here today."

"She was here about an hour ago. She has a gift shop in town, and she wants to carry my mix! She gave me her business card and asked me to contact her!"

"That's so exciting!"

Preoccupied with their discussion, they failed to notice the elderly man walking their way.

"So this is how you intend to support yourself?" Ethan Beaumont asked. He stood before the almost empty folding table under the EZ-UP. Scattered atop the table were a few of Lexi's business cards. He picked one up and looked at it briefly, before tossing it back on the table.

"Grandfather," Lexi greeted tonelessly. Whatever joy and excitement she had expressed a moment ago dissolved.

"She is doing very well!" Angie said angrily, feeling protective.

Lexi reached over and touched her friend's hand; silently signaling she wanted to handle this herself. "Angie, this might be a good time for you to check out the other vendors, like you wanted to do. I'd like to talk to my grandfather alone."

Glaring at Ethan Beaumont, Angie gave her friend a little nod and then walked away, leaving Lexi alone with her grandfather.

"Lexi, perhaps I was hasty in taking away your car and computer."

"What about my clothes and personal items?"

"I'll buy you new clothes," he told her.

"What are you saying, Grandfather?"

"I want you to come home with me. I plan to leave before nightfall tonight and head back to California. I want you to come with me."

"Why would I do that?"

"I'll buy you a new car. Whatever you want," Ethan said calmly, betraying no emotion.

"I'm not marrying Jerome."

He did his best to conceal his irritation and continued, keeping his tone steady and calm. "We don't have to discuss that now."

"Exactly why do you want me to come back with you?"

"What kind of a question is that? You're my granddaughter."

"But you kicked me out of your house and then did everything you could to make it difficult for me to make it on my own. You hired someone to follow me."

"I agree; hiring Barnett was a mistake."

"Kicking me out wasn't?"

"Lexi," he no longer was able to conceal his irritation. "I was trying to teach you a lesson, for your own good. You've always been such a foolish girl, a dreamer just like your father. Just look at what you're doing now! You move to some little town in the middle of the desert and plan to support yourself by selling some silly little hot fudge mix.

"From what my private investigator tells me, you hopped into Barnett's bed after knowing him for just a couple of days. Something that I hope to hell your little friend Angie can keep quiet about, if I ever hope to get you securely married to someone who can take care of you. Fortunately for you, Barnett is bound by a confidentiality agreement, and I doubt he will be foolish enough to make your little affair public. If necessary, I can pay him off to keep him quiet. I imagine he will appreciate the money now that he doesn't have a job. You should appreciate all that I'm willing to do for you!"

"Grandfather, you really don't think much of me, do you?" Lexi asked in a faint whisper.

"What do you mean? You're my granddaughter. I cared enough about you to make sure you were raised properly and received an education. And I'm willing to give you a second chance now. I don't understand what you're asking."

"For one thing, you don't think I'm very smart, do you?"

"Smart? Lexi, you're a girl. You really don't need to be smart to get by in this world. Fortunately for you, you are extremely attractive. But looks don't last forever, so don't expect to rely on them indefinitely."

"Wow," Lexi said, somewhat dazed. "I guess I am a bit stupid. I never truly appreciated the extent of your disregard."

"What are you talking about?"

"I won't be going back with you. I don't need you to buy me a car, or to find me a suitable husband. I don't need anything from you."

"Lexi, this is getting tedious," Ethan snapped. "I'm losing my patience with you. And I'm not going to continue discussing this in the middle of a ridiculous swap meet. I'm going back to the rental house, and I plan to leave before nightfall. If you aren't there before I leave, then I'm finished with you for good. I'll visit my attorney in the morning and change my will. You won't get a dime of my money."

Without waiting for an answer, Ethan turned abruptly and walked away. Speechless, Lexi watched the old man disappear into the crowd.

"So, what happened?" Angie asked thirty minutes later when she returned to the booth. She found Lexi sitting in one of the camp chairs behind the folding table.

"I gave out my last business card. You want to pack it up?"

"Sure. But, what about your grandfather? What did he say?"

"Well, I learned something interesting."

"What's that?"

"Apparently, I was in his will. I assumed he'd disinherited me when he threw me out of his house."

"What do you mean, *was* in his will?"

"He tells me if I don't go back to California tonight, then he'll see his attorney in the morning and disinherit me. Like I said, I thought he'd already done that. He plans to leave by dark."

"So, what are you going to do?"

"I thought maybe we could pack up, go out for an early dinner and maybe catch a show or two."

"You don't want to go back to the house?"

"Nope. Not until after dark."

"Do you need any money?" Jane Barnett asked her son. She sat in the kitchen of her Portland, Oregon, home, talking to Jeff on the telephone.

"No, I have some savings." Jeff sat in his living room in Southern California. It was Monday morning, and he was preparing to return the rental car when his mother called. She hadn't talked to him for several weeks and had no idea what had been going on in his life. Needing to talk to someone, he told her everything.

"So, what are your plans? You know, you can always come home and stay here and look for a job."

"Thanks, Mom. I'm not sure what I'm going to do yet."

"I imagine you could file something against your ex-boss, for wrongful termination. I don't think what he pressured you to do is legal under California employment laws."

"Probably not, but do I really want to sue my ex-employer? I can't imagine that will look great to potential employers."

"Now you sound like your father. You're probably right. But it makes me so mad!"

Jeff smiled. There was something comforting about having parents always there for him, with unconditional love and support. It was something Lexi hadn't had in years.

"You would like her, Mom."

"What about you? Sounds like you're pretty crazy about her."

"Lexi's special. It's not just that she's beautiful—but she is. Beautiful, I mean. She is also smart and creative. I felt comfortable with her in a way I never felt with anyone else. She was completely different than I had imagined."

"What do you mean?"

"The way Beaumont described his granddaughter —before I met her—was that she was rather simple, another spoiled society girl whose big accomplishment in life would be marrying the right man."

"Not really someone I see you with."

"Exactly. But she is nothing like that. There's a portrait of her in the lobby of her grandfather's office. At first, I naturally assumed it was there for the typical reasons you hang a picture of a family member: love, pride. But now, I suspect the portrait was simply another possession on display. A work of art. The artist who painted the portrait is fairly renowned. I bet Beaumont was more impressed by the artist than the subject."

"This former boss of yours doesn't sound very nice."

"No, he isn't."

"Jeff, that part about her inheritance. You said those friends of hers insisted her parents left her something, but she says her grandfather contradicts that. How does she know her grandfather was telling the truth, considering all his lies and manipulations?"

"Beaumont contested the guardianship in court, so I would imagine anything left to her in a will would come under the scrutiny of the court. If there was really any money from her parents, I don't see how he could hide that."

"He could hide it in plain sight."

"I don't understand what you mean."

"Jeff, remember how your father and I put money away each month into a tax-differed savings account for you?"

"Sure. I used that money to go to college."

"With those kinds of accounts, once we put money into it, it belonged to you. Your father and I weren't free to take the money out without a good reason."

"I still don't get what you're saying."

"When you turned eighteen, you could have spent the money however you wanted, and we wouldn't have been able to do a thing about it."

"Yeah, but I used it for college."

"True. But had you wanted to spend it on something else, we couldn't have stopped you."

"I still don't get your point."

"What would have happened if your father and I never told you about the account? It would still be there; it would be your money to spend. But how would you spend it if you didn't know it existed?"

"Are you saying there might be money out there that belongs to Lexi, but she simply doesn't know about it?"

"Who's been in her life to tell her? Her grandfather certainly wouldn't, if he wants a way to control her. Considering the affairs of our social service these days, I don't imagine there is some court clerk or judge waiting for the granddaughter of a wealthy and influential businessman to come of age so they can tell her about her inheritance. Those people have probably moved on."

"I didn't really consider that. I just figured, if Lexi was so certain…"

"Just something to think about."

When Jeff finally said goodbye to his mother, he found it difficult to think about anything else. *Did Lexi have an inheritance she didn't know about?* Before he moved on with his own life, he needed to make some restitution to Lexi. If her grandfather had lied to her about her parents' will, he was determined to find out.

***

LEXI EXPERIENCED A HECTIC WEEK. THE STORE FROM which she normally purchased the Mason jars was out of stock. Apparently, there wasn't a big demand for canning jars in Lake Havasu City, Arizona—until Lexi's arrival. She solved her jar dilemma and moved to the next fire.

On Tuesday, she met with the woman from the local gift shop and settled on a discount case price for resale. Tuesday afternoon another gift shop contacted her—this one located in Sedona, Arizona—who wanted to stock the mix. Apparently, the daughter of the Sedona shop owner had visited Havasu and brought a jar back to Sedona.

Facebook likes were growing hourly on the hot fudge page, and visitors were leaving positive comments. One person asked if Lexi planned to make a sugar-free version of the fudge. Lexi wasn't sure how that would taste, so she stopped by the store and picked up some sugar substitute and made a small batch.

After a bit of experimenting, she discovered cooking the sugar free version in the microwave reacted like overcooked fudge, in that the powdered ingredients formed a hard clump in a pool of oily liquid. It wasn't possible to cook the mix in the microwave for the time required to make the hot fudge sauce, without it becoming rock hard. She tried cooking it on the stove, in the traditional manner. It cooked quicker than the sugar version, and while it tasted okay, for sugar free, it never obtained the original recipe's caramel consistency.

Lexi remembered what Jeff had told her about responsible growth and warning her against trying to grow the business too fast. She missed talking to him about the hot fudge venture and sharing ideas. Wondering what Jeff would say about producing sugar-free hot fudge mix at this time, she intuitively knew the answer. For the moment, she was busy enough producing and marketing the original recipe. There would be time later to expand and bring a sugar-free version to her customers.

By Saturday morning, she was in a panic. Her email box was full with requests for the mix, each one asking her to reserve a jar for Sunday. It had been a challenge packing 48 jars of the mix, along with the folding table, two camp chairs and EZ-UP into Angie's Volkswagen the previous Sunday. As it was, Angie had a photo shoot Sunday afternoon, so she would have to drop Lexi off at the swap meet in the morning and pick her up later in the afternoon. If the photo shoot went on too long, Lexi might end up sitting alone in the London Bridge Shopping Center parking lot, waiting for her ride, after the rest of the vendors left for the day. It also meant it would be impossible to go to the restroom without leaving the booth unattended. She was beginning to feel over-whelmed.

Alone at the house, pacing back and forth in the living room, Lexi tried to decide how to deal with the email requests. *Can I fit that many jars in the car? If I reserve the jars I have, what happens if no one picks them up, and I lose sales?* Lexi wished Angie were home so she would have someone to talk to, but her friend had gone to the store.

Had Angie been home, Lexi might not have asked her opinion anyway. While Angie had been support-ive, she made it clear the hot fudge venture was Lexi's baby and passion—it was not Angie's. Lexi told herself she needed to stop imposing on Angie and learn to manage her new business on her own.

In the midst of her pacing, a knock came at the door. Before opening it, Lexi looked out the peep-hole. To her surprise, it was Jeff. Standing on the front porch wearing denim jeans and a black jacket, he held a large manila envelope in his hands. His fingers fidgeted nervously with the edge of the envelope.

Her heart swelled and pulse accelerated. Instead of the anger she once felt, she was elated to see him again. Although she wanted nothing more than to open the door and leap into his arms, she took a deep breath and calmly opened the door.

"Jeff," Lexi greeted in an even and steady tone.

Since turning off Highway 40 onto Highway 95 en route to Lake Havasu City, Jeff's own heart began beating faster. Standing in Lexi's doorway, he wondered briefly if she could hear its rapid pounding. Jeff's gaze swept over Lexi. She looked even more beautiful than he remembered. Grateful she wasn't slamming the door in his face, he smiled softly.

"Hi, Lexi. I need to talk to you. It's very important."

"I thought you left Havasu."

"I did. I just drove in now."

Lexi glanced over his shoulder and noticed the car parked in the driveway. It was the vehicle he had been driving when spying on her at the Hillcrest Apartments.

"Sure. Come in." Lexi opened the door wider and stood to the side. Jeff followed Lexi into the house. They were both nervous.

"Can we sit down?" Jeff asked.

"Sure." Lexi led him into the living room. She sat on the couch. Nervous and anxious, wondering what he had to say to her and why he had driven so far to say it, she felt as if a hundred butterflies were fluttering about in her stomach.

He placed the envelope on the coffee table and sat

on the love seat. "Lexi, I know you can't forgive me," he began.

"Who said I can't forgive you?" Lexi blurted out.

Stunned, Jeff said nothing but just stared for a moment. "I just assumed…" he stammered.

"Did you mean what you wrote in your note?"

"Yes, every word."

"I've missed you, Jeff," Lexi confessed. Folding her hands together, she tapped her feet nervously against the floor and desperately attempted to contain her emotions.

"I've missed you, too." Jeff smiled. He hadn't expected this, but he certainly wasn't going to complain.

Unable to contain herself, she leapt from the couch and rushed at Jeff. She barely gave him time to open his arms, yet he managed to in spite of her eagerness. Falling together on the small loveseat, Jeff welcomed her kisses, holding her tight.

When the kissing stopped, they lay together on the loveseat, Jeff holding her in his arms.

"This isn't why I came," Jeff murmured, without considering how the words might sound. Lexi tried to pull away, but he refused to let her go.

"You aren't getting away from me," Jeff growled. "I didn't think you'd forgive me. Had I any idea you'd give me this greeting, I would have driven faster to get here." He hugged her tighter, and she stopped struggling.

"Then, why did you come?" Lexi asked, snuggling into his embrace.

"I thought you needed to know. You are a rich woman, Lexi Beaumont."

Lexi frowned and then pulled away slightly, looking down at Jeff.

"What are you talking about?"

"I don't understand." Lexi sat up, as did Jeff. They sat side by side on the loveseat.

"Your grandfather lied about there being no inheritance. Carolyn was right; there was life insurance, plus the proceeds from your family home. There was also the sale of your parents' business and other assets."

"I don't understand. Grandfather said that went to pay off my father's loan."

"Lexi, I don't know about any loan from your grandfather; there's no record of it. And frankly, I seriously doubt there ever was one. You were right; your parents were having financial problems, and your dad did have to borrow some money, but it wasn't from your grandfather."

"I still don't understand."

"Your father had key man insurance, which basically paid off any outstanding debts of his business when he died and made it possible to sell the business at a profit. Plus, they had life insurance on both of them, with you as the benefactor."

"Grandfather said there was no money."

"I did considerable sleuthing this past week. I talked to one person who worked for the courts back then and is retired now. He remembered the case and told me one of your grandfather's arguments for custody was that he would financially support you and promised to give you an education if he was guardian. He also promised the courts he wouldn't touch your inheritance to do so, something the Mannings probably wouldn't have been able to do."

"So, where's the money now?"

"It's in a bank account, waiting for you."

"Why didn't anyone tell me?"

"I imagine they all assumed it was your grandfather's place to explain it all to you. They had no reason to believe he would lie. Plus, the way it's set up, you couldn't touch it until your twenty-first birthday, anyway."

"That was just a few months ago."

"Exactly."

"Well, how much are we talking?" Lexi never considered there was actually an inheritance. For years, her grandfather had told her the opposite. She would have never investigated on her own.

"Are you sitting down?"

Lexi rolled her eyes at his silly question, considering they were both sitting on the loveseat together.

"Almost five million."

"No." Lexi shook her head in disbelief.

"Yes." Jeff nodded.

"How is that even possible?"

"Your parents had a big life insurance policy, both of them. The house sold for even more than what Joe estimated. After your father borrowed that money, his business took a turn for the better and it sold for some major cash after he died. There were also some stocks, minor assets, and over the years, interest earned." Jeff reached to the coffee table, picked up the envelope and handed it to her. "It's all in here. All the details."

"I don't know what to say," Lexi held the large envelope, without looking inside. "I guess I was wrong about my grandfather."

"Excuse me?"

"I know my grandfather isn't good with personal relationships, and I wondered why he even bothered taking me in, considering how he's treated me over the years. But I guess, in his own way, he must have cared, since he made sure my inheritance stayed intact, and he paid for my education and supported me all these years."

Jeff closed his eyes for a moment, reminding himself to maintain his cool. Opening them again, he reached out and took Lexi's free hand in his.

"I wish I could agree with you, Lexi. But remember, he lied to you about it all these years."

"I know, but there must be a reason he did all this." She sounded like a little girl.

"Lexi, I need to tell you the rest." He continued to hold her hand, his expression solemn.

"What?"

"I can't say for certain why your grandfather initially took you in, or why he exploited the angle of preserving your inheritance as a reason for granting him custody."

"Exploited? I don't know what you mean?"

"Lexi, while he may have done what he promised—gave you support and education without touching your inheritance—you can't ignore the fact he's done his best to keep you from knowing about that inheritance."

"I know. But that doesn't make sense. Maybe, in his own strange way, he was protecting me."

"From what? You?"

"Well, he doesn't think I'm very smart." She sounded embarrassed at the admission.

"And he's an idiot," Jeff snapped. "Lexi, you need to understand that your grandfather's behavior is not a reflection on you. A normal person would be proud to have you as a granddaughter."

"There's more, isn't there?"

"Yes. Like I said, I have no idea what his original motivations were when he fought for custody. I spent a lot of time with him the last two years and probably know him better than most. He's very possessive. I wish I could say grandfatherly love inspired him to fight for you, but I suspect it had more to do with stubborn pride. There was no way Ethan Beaumont was going to let strangers raise his granddaughter."

Lexi said nothing, but knew what he was saying was true.

"I also made a call to one of my close friends who still works at your grandfather's company. When I told him what happened, why I was let go, he was pretty pissed. It didn't take much to convince him to do a little snooping for me. I took the information he gave me, pieced it together with a few things I already knew, and called in a few favors from someone who works at one of the banks your grandfather uses. His company is in serious financial difficulty."

"That is impossible."

"I'm afraid not. A few things happened on that last Europe trip that had me wondering, but he's good at making the world see what he wants them to see."

"How serious?"

"At the moment, you have about five million more dollars than he does."

"Grandfather, broke?"

"Unless he can pull some rabbit out of the hat. And frankly, I think you were that rabbit."

"You think he was trying to get his hands on my money to save his company?"

"I'm not really sure if that would be enough to bail him out, but knowing your grandfather, he would go down spending your last dime if he thought there was a chance to save his precious company."

"Jeff, this doesn't make any sense. If he wanted my money, why wouldn't he just come to me and ask? Hell, he could have made up some cover story about why he concealed the inheritance, such as he wanted to surprise me."

"Do you even know your grandfather? Do you honestly think he wants to owe you a favor? I couldn't get anyone at the bank to talk to me about your account, but I found out the general manager had been let go several weeks ago, so I tracked him down, and he was more than willing to talk for a price."

"You paid someone?"

Jeff shrugged and then continued with his explanation. "A while back, your grandfather went to the bank, supposedly on your behalf. He told them you were getting married soon, and you wanted to put your husband on the account and that he was going to be handling your money. He told them you wanted to know what needed to be done to set this up. When asked why you didn't come in, he just laughed and said his granddaughter couldn't be bothered with such mundane tasks."

"All this marrying Jerome business was so those two could get hold of my inheritance?" No longer making excuses for her grandfather, Lexi felt anger mount.

"I think so."

"So, once I married Peters, it would be easier for them to extort my inheritance."

"I think that's what they believed."

"But, why did my grandfather ever believe he could get me to marry his business partner?"

"There is only one reason I can think of."

"What's that?"

"He has no idea who you are."

"I need you," Lexi told Jeff an hour later. Nude, the two lay under the sheets in Lexi's bed, exhausted after a vigorous lovemaking session. Jeff held Lexi in his arms and kissed the top of her head."

"I'm here for you, babe."

Lexi rolled out of his arms and looked at him. "No, I need you to help me with my hot fudge venture."

Jeff frowned at her statement, and she laughed.

"Well, I need you here too." She moved back in his arms. "But, you once offered to work with me long term, and Jeff, I could really use your help."

"I'm happy to see you're moving forward with the hot fudge venture, in spite of the fact that you don't really have to."

"I want to build something, Jeff."

"You're your father's daughter." He chuckled.

"What do you mean?"

"When playing detective this past week, I learned a lot about your father. After he graduated from college, he brought your mother home to meet your grandfather. When your father wouldn't break up with her, he was kicked out—like you were when you refused to marry Peters. Like you, your father didn't sit around and moan about his change of fortune. With your mother, he built a nice little business. You're doing the same thing."

Lexi smiled and snuggled into his embrace.

"I'd like it to be a working partnership," Jeff said.

"I think that could be arranged."

"I've got some money I could invest."

"We don't need your money, I have the inheritance."

"No, Lexi. Let's keep the hot fudge venture separate and treat it like a real business—like it is. As for your inheritance, that's your personal money. As for me, I love you, but I need you to know I'm here for you, not for your money."

Lexi rolled over and faced Jeff. Their noses were just a breath apart. She wrapped her arms around his neck and brushed a kiss over his lips.

"I love you, too, Jeff."

"Hot damn!" Angie stood at the doorway looking into Lexi's bedroom.

"Oh, I guess we should've shut the door." Lexi giggled as she pulled up the sheet to cover their bodies.

"Hi, Angie." Jeff waved from the bed.

"I thought that was your car in the drive. You're blocking me, you asshole." Angie chuckled.

"You still pissed at me?" Jeff asked.

"Just for parking in the driveway. I'm cool with the rest. Glad to see you're back. Does this mean I don't have to wake up at five in the morning and go to that damned swap meet?"

"Yeah, you're off the hook. I'll be taking Lexi."

"Great. Just for that, I'll let you crash at the house until Lexi feels compelled to kick you out... if that ever happens." Angie pulled the door shut, giving her friends privacy as she walked to the kitchen.

It wasn't until an hour later, after Lexi and Jeff dressed and went to the kitchen to get something to eat, that they told Angie about the inheritance. Angie displayed far more outward excitement over the news than Lexi had. She danced around the kitchen, first on her right foot and then her left, flapped her arms like a deranged bird and kept shouting *hot damn!*

To celebrate, Angie offered to take them all out for dinner. Since it was Saturday, Angie called ahead and made a reservation at Angelina's Italian Kitchen. When the bill came, both Jeff and Lexi offered to pay, but Angie refused.

SUNDAY SALES WERE EVEN BETTER THAN THE PREVIOUS week. Another local merchant, wanting to carry the hot fudge mix, approached Lexi. By the time they got home Sunday, both were exhausted. The previous night, Lexi and Jeff had decided to head back to California on Monday, so they went to bed early.

Before leaving Monday morning, Jeff called an old friend of his, an attorney in Los Angeles. Calling in a favor, Jeff convinced his friend to squeeze Lexi in Monday afternoon. She wanted to discuss the best way to go about claiming her inheritance and needed advice on how to manage the funds. She also wanted him to draw up a will.

When they got into Los Angeles Monday afternoon, they had just enough time to grab a hamburger at a fast food restaurant, before making the appointment. By Tuesday, Lexi had access to her funds. She wanted to buy a car, but decided to wait until they got back to Lake Havasu City. If she purchased one in California, they would have to drive back in separate cars.

They spent Wednesday visiting the malls, clothes shopping for Lexi. Although she had gotten her old clothes back when Jeff brought the boxes, it had been over a year since she had purchased anything new for her wardrobe, aside from the thrift shop.

On the way back to Jeff's apartment, they stopped and picked up Chinese food. Both were exhausted and planned to leave for Havasu in the morning, on Valentine's Day.

"What are you going to do about this apartment?" Lexi asked as she opened the cartons of Chinese food.

"I haven't really thought about it."

"I'd like to stay in Havasu, at least until the swap meet ends for the season, which is sometime in May."

"I sort of figured that." Jeff helped himself to some cashew chicken and chow mien. They each took a plate of food and chopsticks with them into the living room and sat together on the couch.

"I really like your apartment, and it's nice to have someplace to stay when we come into town. Why don't you let me pay the rent?"

"I can't have you do that."

"Why not? Consider it a business expense."

"I'm okay for now. But you're probably right. It would be nice to have someplace to crash when we come into town. At least until we figure out where we plan to go in May."

"You know, maybe instead of a car, I should buy a motorhome."

"Motorhome?"

"Sure, we could travel around the country,

promote the hot fudge mix. I'd love to see more of the country. I never did much traveling after my parents died."

"Seriously? You've gone to Europe, haven't you?"

"Nope. I've never been out of the country. And the only time I went to Hawaii was with my parents."

"I guess that surprises me, considering the number of times I had to travel abroad for your grandfather's company."

"Do you really think he's that broke?"

"From what I learned last week, I think he's running on fumes. He even took out a loan on his estate."

"You mean his house?"

"Yes, and considering the amount he borrowed, he has little if any equity left in the property. He's liquidated most of his assets in the last twelve months. It's funny how people see just what they want to see, or expect to see. Now that I look back at certain events that went on over the last couple of years, I should have known the company had serious problems. I knew there were some issues, but I just assumed it was the economy. I figured liquidating some of the properties was a strategy to weed out the dead wood, make the corporation lean and more able to sustain any bumps in the road."

"Well, in your defense, you were fresh out of college."

Jeff was about to tell her she was sweet when the doorbell rang.

"I wonder who that is." Jeff set his plate on the coffee table and stood up. "I bet it's one of the neighbors. I've pretty much been M.I.A. for weeks."

When Jeff opened the front door, he was surprised to find Ethan Beaumont in the doorway.

"Is my granddaughter here?" he demanded. Before Jeff could answer, Ethan pushed his way into the apartment and started shouting, "Lexi! Lexi!"

"What are you doing here?" Lexi asked, standing up from the couch.

"Why are you here with Barnett? He's just using you to get to your money."

"Gee, Grandfather, about that money. Nice of you to tell me I had an inheritance."

"It was for your own good! I was afraid you would do something irresponsible, and look, I was right! Here you are in this man's apartment, and he's cleaned out your bank account!"

"He hasn't touched my bank account, or even tried. Too bad I can't say the same about you."

"I didn't touch a dime of that money," her grandfather insisted.

"No, but you told the bank I was getting married, and you wanted to put my husband in charge of my inheritance."

"I just thought Peters would be better equipped to manage your inheritance. You have no experience handling that kind of money. It wasn't as if we planned to touch it before you were married."

"I think you should worry more about managing your own finances, rather than mine."

"I don't know what you mean."

"I know about the house." It always felt odd to Lexi to call it a house. In reality, it was a mansion. "I understand it's mortgaged to the hilt. You've been selling off your assets. Your company is drowning, and you thought my inheritance might bail you out."

"Don't be ridiculous. In the scheme of things, your inheritance is a drop in the bucket."

"I believe that, Grandfather. I also believe you were fully prepared to drain every last drop for the remote possibility it might save your company."

Ethan Beaumont said nothing. In that moment, he reminded Lexi of a statue that was about to crumble. Without saying another word, he turned and walked from the apartment, closing the door behind him.

Lexi and Jeff silently stared at the closed door. Finally Jeff spoke.

"Are you alright, babe?"

"I wanted to love that man. I wanted him to love me. But I don't see it ever happening, and he is the only family I have left in the world."

Jeff gathered Lexi up in his arms and held her tightly.

Closing her eyes, she leaned into his chest and wrapped her arms around him.

"You have me and Angie. And when you meet my family, you can have them, too. They will love you, Lexi."

"I love you, Jeff Barnett."

The housekeeper was beginning to worry about her employer. Ethan Beaumont had been sitting in his study for over an hour, staring blankly across the room. Sitting in a wingback chair, his elbows propped on the chair's arms, he tapped his chin with his knuckles, his fingers laced together.

She couldn't help but feel sorry for him. After all, he was an old man and alone. It had been almost three years since he had seen his granddaughter, but the housekeeper couldn't really fault the girl. He had driven her away.

He should be proud of the young woman, considering what she had accomplished in the last few years. Thinking he would want to read the article about Lexi that appeared in the recent *People Magazine*, she had brought it to him. His eyes only skimmed the article before he tossed the magazine aside as if it held no interest to him.

Lexi and her husband's Walt's Hot Fudge on Demand had become a phenomenal success. They were no longer manufacturing the product in her kitchen, but had opened a plant in Lake Havasu City, Arizona, and they were distributing the hot fudge mix throughout the country. According to the article, they had recently turned down a lucrative buyout by a major food corporation.

Ethan Beaumont's year had not gone so well. There was nothing left of his company; it had gone so quickly. Things had accelerated when Jerome Peters embezzled what was left of any liquid assets and disappeared.

All that he had left was the house, which really was not his. The bank had foreclosed on the property weeks earlier and had already sold it to an investor. They informed him the new owner was willing to let him stay in the mansion temporarily and offered to pay for the household staff, since they wanted the estate properly maintained. It was an offer he couldn't afford to refuse.

They were letting him keep his personal belongings, but the things of real value, such as art, had been sold months ago. That morning, a representative from the bank had called and told him they were coming over that afternoon and bringing the new owner. He assumed they were coming over with the eviction notice.

He had social security, which was a pittance, considering his previous lifestyle. Selling what remained of the household furniture would net him a little cash, but not much. If he were a younger man, he would see this as a challenge and make another fortune. But, he was eighty-four and no longer possessed the necessary youth required for rebuilding dynasties. For the first time in Ethan Beaumont's life, he was afraid.

"You have visitors," the housekeeper said, interrupting his thoughts. Ethan glanced up.

"Show them in," he told her, wondering why she seemed so cheerful with the news of visitors, as if she thought it was someone he would actually be happy to see.

A few minutes later, the housekeeper showed the new arrivals to the study and then hastily departed the room. When Beaumont glanced up, to see who had walked in, he visibly tensed. It was Lexi and the representative from the bank. The man was grinning, as if he, like the housekeeper, thought Ethan should be thrilled with their company.

"What are you doing here?" Ethan asked, his voice gruff.

"She's the one who bought the property," the banker explained.

"What kind of trick is this?"

A flicker of confusion crossed the banker's face. He assumed Beaumont would be thrilled to know Lexi was the new owner, and he wouldn't have to move.

"Can you please leave my grandfather and I alone? We need to talk."

The banker gave a little nod and hastily departed, not wanting to stick around for longer than necessary, considering the surly nature of the elderly man.

With measured calm, Lexi walked to her grandfather and gave him a perfunctory kiss on the forehead, then sat on the empty wingback chair next to his.

"You look well, Grandfather. I understand Peters has disappeared."

"Did you come here to gloat?"

"No. I guess that was cruel of me. Sorry. No, I came here to tell you I've bought this house, and you don't have to move. I'll continue to pay all the household expenses, such as the utilities, insurance, and household staff. I'll give you a monthly allowance to cover your food and other expenses."

"Why would you do that?" he snapped.

"You did it for me."

"What are you talking about?"

"When my parents were killed, you gave me a safe place to live. You paid for my room, board, all of my expenses. You paid for my education. Now it's my turn to repay the favor."

"I don't want your charity," he snapped.

"It isn't charity, Grandfather. It's what family is supposed to do. Family is supposed to take care of each other."

"What do you want in exchange?" he asked suspiciously.

"I don't want anything at all. Tell me grandfather, what did you want when you took me in after my parents died?"

"What do you mean, what did I want? You had nothing I wanted; you were just a child."

"What about my inheritance?"

"I didn't need your money back then, and even if I had, I couldn't touch it." He sounded insulted.

"So, you took me in because I was family?" she prodded.

He didn't answer immediately. "I suppose so," he finally conceded.

Lexi smiled and stood up. She walked to her grandfather's side, leaned over and placed a light kiss on his forehead.

"And that is exactly the same reason I'm doing it, Grandfather."

Lexi turned from him and walked from the room. She wondered if he would call out to her, say anything, but he didn't. He just watched her leave.

"You okay?" Jeff asked when Lexi got in the car with him a few minutes later.

"Yeah, I think I am," Lexi smiled. She closed the car door and buckled the seat belt.

"I love you Lexi." Jeff told her as he turned on the ignition.

"I know, Jeff. I love you, too.

WALT'S HOT FUDGE ON DEMAND RECIPE

Dry Mix

In a glass jar combine:

2 cups sugar

1/3 cup powdered milk

6 tablespoons unsweetened cocoa

2 teaspoons powdered vanilla

Dash salt

Place a lid on the jar and shake to mix well.

Single Serving Hot Fudge Sauce

In an 8-ounce glass Pyrex measuring cup put:

1 tablespoon butter

1 tablespoon water

Microwave for 40 seconds.

Add 2 tablespoons dry mix to the butter and water mixture.

Stir with a knife to blend. Avoid splashing choco-late on the inside of the glass.

Microwave for 42 seconds. Let sit 5-10 minutes before pouring over ice cream.

*Cooking time will vary if cooked in a different sized container or a non-glass container

Where readers first met Lexi
Sundered Hearts

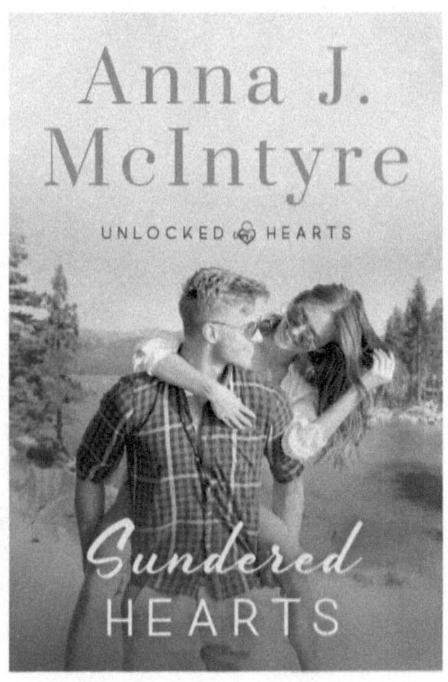

Susan Thomas thought she had it all—a home, a husband she loved, and children in her future—until everything came crashing down one rainy afternoon, exposing her perfect world as a lie.

Determined to move on with her life, Susan recklessly drags Brandon Carpenter from the bar and into her bed. When she doesn't see him again, Susan fears she is repeating her same old mistakes.

Seeking refuge at Shipley Mountain, the last person Susan expects to run into is Brandon. He has his own reasons for being on the mountain. Brandon and Susan must put aside their misunderstandings. A child's life is at stake.

After Sundown

Women don't come to After Sundown for the beer – they come to get laid. When wealthy Cole Taylor walks into the bar that night, it's for a drink. He gave up one-night stands in his wild youth, but that changes when he sees her. She is too tempting to pass up, and by the looks from the other men at the bar, he needs to move quick to claim the prize.

Kit Landon - a struggling young widow, raising her daughter alone - has her own reasons for being at After Sundown. And it has nothing to do with illicit sex. But things can escalate a little too fast after nervously downing several beers on an empty stomach.

The conservative young widow finds herself in an

extremely compromising situation and barely manages to escape, leaving behind a furious Cole Taylor.

Kit never wants to see the man again, but she is in for a big surprise.

While Snowbound

Snowbound with the famous rocker might be her best friend's fantasy, but it isn't Ella's. Nor is she impressed with the fact Brady Gates was voted sexiest man of the year—twice. Ella was looking forward to the isolation of her mountain cabin and the peace and quiet she needs to finish writing her book. Rescuing the careless celebrity in the midst of a blizzard and taking him to the safety of her remote cabin was not how she intended to spend her time on the mountain.

Weary of lovestruck fans climbing into his bed uninvited and the ever-present paparazzi, Brady Gates had planned to take an incognito break from his hectic life and spend several weeks alone at a remote mountain cabin.

Finding himself stranded in a blizzard doesn't bother him half as much as the fact the one woman he wants is the one woman who is the least interested in him.

HAUNTING DANIELLE

THE GHOST OF MARLOW HOUSE

THE GHOST WHO LOVED DIAMONDS

THE GHOST WHO WASN'T

THE GHOST WHO WANTED REVENGE

THE GHOST OF HALLOWEEN PAST

THE GHOST WHO CAME FOR CHRISTMAS

THE GHOST OF VALENTINE PAST

THE GHOST FROM THE SEA

THE GHOST AND THE MYSTERY WRITER

THE GHOST AND THE MUSE

THE GHOST WHO STAYED HOME

THE GHOST AND THE LEPRECHAUN

THE GHOST WHO LIED

THE GHOST AND THE BRIDE

THE GHOST AND LITTLE MARIE

THE GHOST AND THE DOPPELGANGER

THE GHOST OF SECOND CHANCES

THE GHOST WHO DREAM HOPPED